Love & Money

DESIGNED TO BE DIFFERENT FIGHTING TO BE THE SAME

RODNEY COX
DON BLANTON

Printed in the United States of America

ISBN 978-1-61658-471-9

9 8 7 6 5 4 3 2 1 0 1 2 3 4 5 6 7 8 9 10

Published by Love and Money Ministries
Scottsdale, Arizona

Unless otherwise stated, all Scripture references are taken from the New International Version (NIV), copyright ©1973, 1978, 1984 by International Bible Society.

"It was because your hearts were hard that Moses wrote you this law," Jesus replied. "But at the beginning of creation God 'made them male and female. 'For this reason a man will leave his father and mother and be united to his wife, and the two will become one flesh. So they are no longer two, but one. Therefore what God has joined together, let man not separate."

—Mark 10:5-9 (NIV)

Rodney Cox is the Founder and President of *Ministry Insights International*, a company dedicated to transforming church, marriage and family relationships worldwide. He is an author, speaker and teacher who has impacted more than 250,000 people around the world. He resides in Scottsdale, Arizona, with his wife Beth.

Don Blanton is the President of *MoneyTrax Inc.*, a company dedicated to the development of innovative communication tools for financial service professionals, designed to transform their client's finances. He and his wife Connie live in Atlanta, Georgia.

Special Thanks

We would like to thank Gordon for his creative writing skills and the countless hours he devoted to this project.

Gordon Adams is Executive Director of *Vision Foundation, Inc.*, a non-profit ministry organization. He is a teacher, speaker, mentor and author, and has ministered in 28 countries around the world. Gordon lives with his wife, Marylyn, in Knoxville, Tennessee.

Foreword

Every couple, no matter how much or how little money they have, struggles over finances. Why? Because money is symbolic of a personality power struggle. It's inevitable. Money causes more tension and turmoil between husbands and wives than any other topic. It's a fact that every marriage counselor can attest to.

That's why we are so glad to see Rodney Cox and the team at Ministry Insights put their heads together on this biblically grounded Love & Money project. We don't know of anyone better suited to tackle this thorny issue in a way that makes it much easier to handle.

Through this book they will teach you to explore your differing approaches to money so that you aren't working against each other, but rather leveraging them to your advantage. Once you learn that secret, your life and your marriage gets a whole lot easier.

We're confident you'll find the help you're looking for in these pages. Rodney, along with Don Blanton have shown us all how to wisely invest our efforts in this important area.

This book is like money in the bank.

Drs. Les & Leslie Parrott
Founders of RealRelationships.com
Authors of Trading Places and L.O.V.E.

Table of Contents

Part I
Different by Design

Chapter 1

Meet the Stuckeys and the Baileys

Beloved, if God so loved us, we ought also to love one another.
—1 John 4:11 (KJV)

But lay up for yourselves treasures in heaven...
—Matthew 6:20 (KJV)

It's 6:00 a.m. An alarm sounds in two households, just as it does in hundreds of thousands of homes across America. Another day is about to begin for two special families whom you will learn to love as we journey with them through the pages of this book. We will laugh with them, cry with them and celebrate with them as they make new discoveries about life, love and money.

Meet the Stuckeys and the Baileys. These two couples are a microcosm of individuals and families we can relate to from our jobs, in our neighborhoods, and in our churches. They are not Fortune 500 couples and they don't live in mansions. These families have not come from wealthy stock—no "silver spoons" are to be found in their backgrounds—and they don't have portfolios that the rest of us might covet. In fact, they look just like you and me.

Meet the Stuckeys

Stu and Dina Stuckey have been married 14 years, and they love each other. They have two children, and they both have good jobs. They have nice cars; they live in an upscale suburban subdivision. By all outward appearances they have arrived—the average middle class American family. However, something isn't right, and they have never been able to put their finger on what it is.

They have struggles—not really "fights"—but it seems their issues are often a reoccurrence of the same old thing. They have financial pressures, and it sometimes creates tensions and discussions that lead to frustration for both of them. Stu "stews"—he's the worrier. Dina is the "dynamo" in their family—always busy, on lots of committees, involved in community affairs and active in their church.

Stu is always asking himself hard questions out of his sense of responsibility: "Will we have enough money to retire?" "Will we have enough money to send our kids to college?" "How long will I have to work before I can retire?" Good questions, right?

Oh, the Stuckeys save. Stu puts some money in his 401k at the office because everyone else is doing it. He would like to have even more withdrawn from his weekly paycheck because he worries that what he is doing won't be enough to secure their future. Dina always reminds him that they cannot afford to save more and assures him things will "all work out." Dina also puts subtle pressure on Stu—she'd like to live it up a little now instead of always hearing that they must save for retirement. Their latest issue was her request for them to take that dream vacation next year. Stu doesn't think they can afford it. Dina's response was, "We're not getting any younger, you know!"

Dina has encouraged Stu to think about finding a new job—one that could put them in a better financial position. Stu thinks more money may be the answer, but he is unwilling to take the risk of leaving the security of his job and starting over. After all, he has two kids to support, future college expenses, and weddings for their two girls to think about. He knows the current lifestyle they enjoy requires both their incomes. They look good. They smell good. But basically they're broke! They're "stuck" in a rut. They have resigned themselves to their present condition and parked their relationship at this comfortable but boring address in life.

They have bought a lie: "This is as good as it will ever get."

Meet the Baileys

Unlike the Stuckeys, Tiger and Kitty Bailey are a twenty-something couple: part of the "now generation." Raised in homes somewhat like the Stuckeys, they feel entitled to start out in life and marriage at the level of their parents and work up from there!

Married four years, with no children, they also both work. They met in college and fell in love without realizing that it was their differences that attracted them to one another. There was chemistry: the sparks flew, and there was the infatuation and romance that our culture equates with love. However some of that has begun to wane as the realities of life, work and marriage have slowly encroached on their relationship.

Tiger is the go-getter of the two; Kitty is the perky, "purr-fect" partner. Tiger "shows well" outside the home—he's the up-front, GQ button down collar, bottom line rational communicator. Kitty is sincere, well liked, and a relational communicator.

Lately they have begun to spend less time together. The unreal expectations they both brought into the marriage are not being met, and they have each resorted to blaming the other for the erosion of intimacy. Their ability to communicate effectively has diminished, and the joy they once felt as newly weds has sadly dissipated. They are so different that they are beginning to wonder if they even like each other and why they ever got married in the first place. To add to this, financial pressures are not helping their marriage. They eat out almost every night of the week and often alone because of their busy schedules. Their credit cards are always at their limit, and they have little discretionary money for unforeseen emergencies. They are still paying off college loans, most of which belong to Kitty. They drive expensive cars that require two large payments each month. They have a $20 start-the-day-habit: the Starbucks drive-through on the way to work. They are the perfect picture of a modern, well-educated, young, ambitious couple, struggling to establish themselves.

Like the Stuckeys, their two-career marriage is very time-consuming. They live in a trendy downtown apartment that they really enjoy. They understand they are pouring money down a rat-hole by renting, but they cannot come up with the down payment for a home. Tiger is aggressively pursuing advancement in his career: climbing the proverbial ladder of success. He was fortunate enough to get the job he really wanted right out of college, and he enjoys the competition of the business world. Like so many of his peers, he believes more is better, and that money and professional advancement will help solve any problems they might encounter.

Kitty, the passive partner, doesn't speak much to Tiger about her fears or desires. She keeps her feelings pretty much to herself. She really wants a house in the country like the one she grew up in, and eventually children, but she doesn't push Tiger. She has learned better. She knows that if they are ever able to have what she wants, it will take more than they are currently making, even with their combined incomes. Lifestyle reduction never seems to occur to either of them. In addition to having no emergency funds, they have no savings other than the small amount they are trying to set aside to make a down payment on a home.

Kitty would like to pay off the credit card and college loans first; Tiger wants to make his mark on the world. Kitty wants a stable home environment, and is not as concerned about outward appearances. Tiger wants all the trappings of success: cars, cash, big house, corner office. Kitty is practical; Tiger is political. They are at what seems to them to be an insurmountable impasse. The only solution the Baileys can see is to—to "bail" out! The growling tiger and the passive pussycat are contemplating an end to it all.

They, too, have bought a lie: "There is simply no hope for our marriage!"

The Truth About Lies

What if what the Stuckeys and the Baileys thought to be true turned out not to be true? When do you think they would want to know? If you can identify at all with either of these two couples, you also may have bought into the same lies in whole or in part. Your ideas of marriage, and your concepts of money management may be a mixture of truth and fiction. If there could be a way out of the traps and pitfalls you might be experiencing, when would YOU want to know? Wouldn't you be anxious to discover and apply sound principles that would strengthen your marriage and start you on the path toward a more secure financial future?

Have you put your life on cruise control, believing "this is as good as it gets; I'm stuck here?" Have you seriously contemplated "bailing out" on your relationship simply because you can't think of any other way of solving your personal and/or financial struggles?

The pairing of Love and Money may at first seem odd. How do they relate? Professional counselors have reported that the two greatest conflicts within marriage revolve around the issues of communication and finance. Conflicts in marriage are inevitable; however, the lack of resolution of either marital or financial conflicts may cause us to feel stuck or to consider bailing out of our marriages.

These two concepts—love and money—should complement one another, not conflict with each other. The pairing is purposeful. There is hope that we can experience significant change both in our marriages and our finances. However we must first *recognize* the lies and then apply the truths that will produce a *transformation*. In this book we will challenge you to take a fresh look at your marriage and your money, and to consider the significant part that God wants to play in this transformational process.

Our Love Affair With Love

To think of marriage is first to think about love. The word itself is laden with misconceptions, brought on by a number of factors. Drawing from deceptive messages, lovers enter into the marriage relationship with unrealistic expectations and thereby seeds of failure are planted. These seeds continue to be watered by pride, self-centeredness, ambition and insensitivity, producing patterns and paradigms not easily changed. We need a clearer understanding of love—love that will build and not break relationships— love that is not built upon misleading messages and deceptions.

The first factor that may deceive us is **the world around us;** the message our media delivers about love is, on one hand, recreational sex, and on the other, romantic fantasy. Consider the Baileys: is there any possibility that either of these deceptions affected them at the time they were married? After all, they experienced the "rush" of romanticism, but that alone seems not to have sustained them. This romantic picture of love can cause anyone to become infatuated with infatuation—in love with love itself.

Flowing out of culture—the world around us—is another factor contributing to the faulty foundations and unrealistic expectations we bring into marriage: *the American dating ritual.* Usually, we "put our best foot forward" during this time—we have a honeymoon before the honeymoon. We take great pains to look good—to make a good impression—and we are usually guarded about our innermost fears and feelings. Thus, if we are unwilling to expose our real selves to one another—to begin to understand our differences—we have little chance of developing a successful marriage. Few couples receive the kind of pre-marital counseling which aims at understanding differences and which encourages celebration of those differences. We want to encourage couples like the Baileys and the Stuckeys to recognize what they each "brought to the party" when they made their vows to each other. Perhaps without realizing it, they have great gifts to offer one another!

A third factor that can deliver a misleading message is *the family/parental behaviors to which we were exposed.* After all, we "reproduce after our own kind," meaning that we tend to mimic behavior modeled by others—in this case, our parents. If the model is flawed, the behavioral patterns we develop for our own marriages could turn out to be defective as well. The Baileys parents, for example, were both divorced, so the model for them was to "bail out" when the going got tough for them. By contrast, the Stuckeys parents believed they should "grind it out," even though their marriage had largely disintegrated. That generation simply did not consider divorce an option, so Stu and Dina have accepted their lot in life, conceding there is little hope for change.

The last, and perhaps most destructive deception, is *our own sin, or self-nature.* The Bible, in 1 John 2:16, says, "For the world offers only the lust for physical pleasure, the lust for everything we see, and the pride in our possessions. These are not from the

Father. They are from this evil world" (NLT). Within the framework of marriage and other relationships, we must deal with issues of unhealthy cravings, the desire to possess things, and our own pride, which expresses itself in so many ways. The "entitlement mentality" of today's generation grows out of this form of arrogance: "I deserve it—you owe it to me."

These sinful passions are alive and well today, and if we continue to pursue them there are consequences. The Scriptures speak of "…visiting the iniquity of the fathers upon the children, and upon the children's children, unto the third and to the fourth generation….." (Exodus 34:7 KJV). The NIV translates this as, "…punishes the children and their children for the sins of the fathers to the third and fourth generations." This is often referred to as "generational sins," pointing to our propensity to reproduce the sinful behaviors of our forebears.

We can conclude, therefore, that both the Baileys and Stuckeys have been deceived by messages that now prevent them from moving on to what God wants for their marriages. The Stuckeys started well. They loved and cherished one another. They placed high value on their relationship, and family activities occupied a prominent place in their value system. Slowly, however, the increased complexity of life and their decreased capacity to deal with their responsibilities brought about a shift within the framework of their marriage. The Baileys simply have been unable to even identify accurately the quandary they are in, and seem to have lost motivation to exert any effort to make their marriage work. Their present course is destined to fail.

Our Love Affair With Wealth

Just as we have a love affair with *love*, we have a love affair with *wealth*.

The culprit is that what we think to be true simply isn't true. Our picture of "truth" about money, just as we have said about marriage, often comes from our culture, our parents, and our own selfish desires, when it ought to come from God. Consider that for decades in Western society, we have been brought up to believe that bigger is better, that quantity is superior to quality. The motto of the day is "get all you can and can all you get." Success measured by the accumulation of wealth is the standard operating procedure in our part of the world. Because of our inclination to compare ourselves with one another, life has become a "giant monopoly game," where we measure our progress using the wrong "score card." Chasing dollars passionately, we disregard the Biblical warning, "...the love of money is the root of all evil..." (1 Tim. 6:10).

Money, as we have stated earlier, is a prominent cause of contention in marriages. The Baileys certainly illustrate this point: striving to succeed, Tiger lost sight of the true objectives of his marriage. He bought the lie: "money will make us happy. As problems arise, I will throw more money at them. I'm certain I will always be able to out-earn our needs." In this book, we want to counter the lies about money with the truth about money. We will explore practical ways to help you manage your resources, and apply these principles in an effort to improve your marriage and financial life.

We humans are so easily infatuated: we carry on love affairs with little knowledge of why. So subtle are the temptations and the hidden lies that we aren't aware of the dangers they pose until they have entwined themselves around our hearts, damaging our ability to see the truth of God's Word.

We have witnessed many spiritual lives being sacrificed on the altar of success: marriages being marred by building them on faulty foundations. Children absorb inaccurate ideas about marriage and money through constant exposure to television, advertising, magazines, the internet and even a simple stroll through the mall. Comparison leads to a lack of contentment, then to covetousness, and finally to competition with one another for what we consider to be limited resources. The lack of role models exhibiting God's design for marriage only perpetuates the problems, and amplifies them in each succeeding generation.

Every person has a worldview. As you consider what you have believed up to this point about love, marriage, relationships, and money issues, ask yourself where you might have derived your definition of the truth. Where did the information come from? For you to understand the truths we are about to impart, you should know that *Love and Money* is based upon these four foundational presuppositions:

1. It is impossible for you to truly love your spouse without the love of Christ.
2. God created differences to complete you, not hinder you.
3. All that you have belongs to God and comes from God.
4. It is God who gives you the ability to acquire wealth.

In the following chapters, we will address many different components of love, marriage, work, wealth, and management of resources. With these presuppositions in mind, our objectives are:

- To increase your understanding of God's divine design for differences
- To increase your understanding of biblical and practical financial truths

Our heart's desire is to strengthen your marriage and help you achieve the unity and oneness that God has intended from the beginning of time.

If what you thought to be true turned out not to be true, when would YOU want to know? We have some valuable insights we want to share with the Stuckeys and the Baileys. If you'd like, feel free to listen in.

Chapter 2

Danger: Differences Ahead!

For this reason a man will leave his father and mother and
be united to his wife, and the two will become one flesh.
—*Ephesians 5:31(NIV)*

Have you ever heard the saying, "If two people think alike, one of them is not necessary?" We may smile at that, but somehow down deep we know there is a ring of truth to it.

The fact is the people we enjoy most are those who act, talk and think like we do.

When it comes to real life, we struggle with our differences— spouses, family, coworkers, and even our closest friends. However, when it comes to *the intimate* part of marriage, we are grateful for differences! Usually, however, those who differ from us bother us— perhaps even irritate us.

In this chapter we want to dialogue with you on the dangers of differences. This chapter will be intentionally instructional. If you hang on, though, we'll get to a fun conversational piece in the next chapter as we get an inside look at some real-life situations and listen in on some conversations with the Stuckeys and the Baileys. Right now, however, let's set the stage: we need a grid or lens through which to peek in on our friends Stu, Dina, Tiger and Kitty.

At the heart of this matter of difference is a crucial principle: *God designed us differently in order to* **complete** *us, not hinder us.* He had a grand purpose in mind. This means we are not meant to *compete* with one another but to *complement* or enhance one another. The definition of "complete" is, "that which brings to perfection." The rub is that many of us judge differences rather than value them. We wrestle with them. We chafe under them. They make us uncomfortable. ("Why can't she do it my way?" or "Why does he do that?") The result is division. It may be slight at the beginning, but the chasm may widen over time.

We need a sign posted right on the door of our hearts before we enter into contact with our spouse: DANGER! DIFFERENCES AHEAD!

Paramount Principle

If you take away anything from this chapter, it should be this:

Only when we learn to value and appreciate differences as God's divine design will we experience the fullness of what God has intended for us from the very beginning of time.

"Genesis" means "beginnings." In the Book of Genesis, which is named in Hebrew, "In the Beginning," God gives this glimpse of his divine design:

> In the beginning God created the heavens and the earth....
> ...so God created man in his own image, in the image of
> God he created him; male and female he created them...
> —Genesis 1:1, 27 (NIV)

It is clear not only that God was in the "creating business," but that he was in the "creating differently" business! He made them male and female. Purposeful planning. This is our first hint that God was cooking up something good for the human race.

Each time God created something, he looked at it and remarked, "...it is good," and, "...it is very good." At one point, by contrast, he stopped and stated:

> The LORD God said, "It is not good for the man to be alone. I will make a helper suitable for him.'"
> —Genesis 2:18 (NIV)

Good; very good; not good. Something wasn't right. Great scenery, wonderful view, and perfect weather—a seemingly ideal world for God's supreme creation, Adam. But this first man was not complete. God's evaluation of Adam's home life was:

He was alone and he needed a helper.

But not just ANY kind of helper; not someone just like him! God didn't *clone* Adam. By God's divine design—his incredible creativity—he came up with this wonderful solution to Adam's "aloneness": a "**suitable** helper." Not just a *helper*. A particular *kind* of helper: one tailor-made just for him. This term, from the 16th century, has its origins in the word "agreeable." The English Standard Version of Genesis 2:18 says, "**fit** for him."

Think of a suit. Who wants a suit that doesn't fit? We usually pay extra to get it to fit correctly (the better the fit, the more expensive the tailoring!). God is a Master Tailor— he goes all out—pays a premium price for the very best fit. His plan is to "make every marriage in heaven" by fashioning the two parts to make a perfect whole.

Nice picture. A real "Kodak moment."

So what happened? WE DID! Resident within the mind and heart of every human being is the ability to make choices: wrong ones or right ones. We have desires and drives, which, if misguided, lead us right up to that sign we mentioned: "DANGER! DIFFERENCES AHEAD." Most of us were attracted to someone very different from ourselves, but we can't seem to come to grips with those differences. (The axiom that "opposites attract" is further validated in our culture one marriage at a time.) One day we seem to be together; the next day (hour? minute?) we're not even on the same page. (Ask anyone married for more than a week!) For many, the awareness of differences began during the honeymoon. *The degree of difference between spouses greatly affects the potential level of conflict within their marriage.*

Over the years Stu and Dina have learned to live with some of their differences, while others they have refused to address. In spite of them, they have "stuck" it out, and have agreed to disagree within the polarity of their relationship. It's a very different story with Tiger and Kitty—they even have "cat" fights over the smallest things. For example, Tiger requires a high degree of neatness in his life. His shaving gear and toothbrush are always in the same place; he even rolls the toothpaste a certain way. Kitty litters her things all over the bathroom with no sense of organization at all—which drives Tiger insane. "Why can't you just put your things away where they belong?" he yells. Meaning, "Why can't you be just be like me—is that so difficult?" *The truth is it is impossible for your spouse to be like you.*

And that's exactly how God intended it! Can you believe that?

Truthfully, most of us are painfully aware of our limitations. We know that humans come in different shapes and sizes. We perceive things differently: what's right for you may not be right for me. What is important to your neighbor or coworker may not be important to you and your family at all! Sometimes we don't even understand our own behavior! Are our motives pure? Are our actions truly altruistic?

The truth is, we all need help. The Stuckeys do, even though on the outside they appear to be reasonably together. The Baileys surely do: they are a microwave-popcorn-marriage waiting to pop! So, where do we turn for answers?

The Truth About Unity in Marriage

Under the floodlight of truth, the deceptions of darkness disappear. Components of the solution to our differences can be found in God's marriage manual, the Bible. God really wants to help us clean up our acts. He is in the relational restoration business. Consider this passage of Scripture:

> The body is a unit, though it is made up of many parts; and though all its parts are many, they form one body. So it is with Christ. For we were all baptized by one Spirit into one body—whether Jews or Greeks, slave or free—and we were all given the one Spirit to drink.
>
> Now the body is not made up of one part but of many. If the foot should say, "Because I am not a hand, I do not belong to the body," it would not for that reason cease to be part of the body. And if the ear should say, "Because I am not an eye, I do not belong to the body," it would not for that reason cease to be part of the body. If the whole body were an eye, where would the sense of hearing be? If the whole body were an ear, where would the sense of smell be? But in fact God has arranged the parts in the body, every one of them, just as he wanted them to be.
>
> —1 Corinthians 12:12-18 (NIV)

In these verses, God gives us a practical picture of wholeness or unity through the metaphor of the human body. This chapter in the Bible is descriptive of what God designed the Body of Christ to become. We can also extend its application to marriages and other relationships. We can derive several insights from this narrative. We will outline four principles that might serve to put some fresh wind in the sails of any marriage.

In the passage above, note the word: UNIT. The theme of these verses is unity. Verse 13 says, "For we were all baptized by **one Spirit** into **one body.**" The church is about unity. Marriage is about unity: togetherness—oneness. Within a marriage, the component parts, or individuals, are to move from independence to interdependence. Fundamentally we need to grasp this truth: *I need you and you need me.* Independence is the path away from God, and it obliterates unity. The final result is **isolation.**

Principle One

God's divine design is intended for different parts to be arranged to produce a whole.

For example, the Baileys—due largely to Tiger's aggressiveness and Kitty's passiveness—are headed in this very direction (more about this later). They are independent parts, living as married singles, each with their own agenda. They are not two living as one, but two living as two. They desperately need to understand how to reverse this trend and move toward one another interdependently.

On the surface, the Stuckeys seem happy enough, but they have become so busy with life and activities that their times together as a couple have become few and far between. They are drifting, the currents of life carrying them further apart. They, too, could end up with a marriage on parallel tracks rather than a single one. Independence becomes an attractive option when the communication that leads to interdependence requires more effort than time seems to allow.

Principle Two

We do not need to strive to become something other than what we are in order to belong.

Remember those unrealistic expectations to which we have referred? How many of those did YOU pack in your suitcase when you went on your honeymoon cruise? Some conniving young spouses actually contemplate changing their mates more to their liking once they have tied the knot! They packed a blueprint in their suitcase!

Cute idiosyncrasies that were part of dating life suddenly become annoyances when the newness of marriage has worn off. What could have prepared them for that?

The Stuckeys, married 14 years, may never have heard of temperament analysis instruments that help people understand how God has wired them. Couples married 20-30 years ago didn't even have access to the literature that has been created since then to help couples grapple with these issues. Stu and Dina certainly are different, but since they parked themselves at "resignation.com," they seem not to want to make any further attempts at growing their relationship.

In our 1 Corinthians verses, we read, "If the foot should say, 'Because I am not a hand, I do not belong to the body,' it would not for that reason cease to be part of the body." Many individuals strive after things God didn't want them to have in order to become something God did not intend them to be. This produces a great deal of stress and frustration. We don't need to change any more than our spouse needs to change. We just need to work harder at becoming who God originally created us to be! That is what it means to belong. "I can't be you, and you can't be me"—that's the essence of diversity within unity.

Principle Three

We do not need people around us who act and think just like we do.

Why do we prefer the company of people who are just like us? Are the best marriages those where the husband and wife are more alike than different? Are the internet marriage and dating sites the best way for everyone to prepare for marriage: testing for every dimension of compatibility? Is the discovery of someone just like you the key to a successful marriage? Is God's design out of line?

It seems easier to surf the waves of life with those who think like us, act like us, etc., doesn't it? Is there really less stress, less conflict and more harmony? Can we just set the cruise control? "I'm okay; you're okay." Right!

The truth about this deception is that it would be impossible to have a cohesive marriage if we were not different. God calculates differently than we do: one+one=one. Diversity and variety is what brings shades of color into the fabric of marriage. (Men, there actually are signals that run through the air that only women can pick up!) So why should we continue trying to mold our partners into replicas of ourselves? We don't appreciate them trying to change us. We all need to loosen up and not take things so seriously! Sometimes differences are quite humorous. It's just plain boring if both husband and wife are the same!

In the 1 Corinthians passage, v. 17 says, "If the whole body were an eye, where would the sense of hearing be? If the whole body were an ear, where would the sense of smell be?" The point of this passage is that our marriages would be aberrations if differences did not exist. As couples we need to learn to value differences, not resist them.

Principle Four

God "sets" or "arranges" the members of his body (and spouses within a marriage) as he wants them to be.

In the Amplified Bible, verse 18 of our passage reads, "But as it is, God has **placed** and **arranged** the limbs and organs in the body, each [particular one] of them, just as He wished and saw fit and with the best adaptation." The New American Standard rendering of "placed" or "arranged" is "set." This is a jeweler's term. Visually picture a ring with a fine stone set in place for all to admire. Just as a jeweler sets a jewel, God sets the members of his Body, the Church, in place. Likewise, he sets, or arranges our mates in place alongside us. The lesson is, obviously, that we don't pick the people around us. God is the Master Jeweler (just as he is the Master Tailor). God, therefore, arranges marriages for the good of both spouses. His desire is to radiate his own beauty through the union, provide protection for them from the surrounding storms of life, and help cover the imperfections of each. Early in marriage, spouses tend to overlook differences; later, however, many exploit one another by calling attention to what they now consider flaws. This is the danger to which we have referred. What has changed? We begin to view one another through the lens of weakness. God's standard is to honor and praise one another, and to embrace differences as his plan to complete us not to hinder us.

David, the "man after God's own heart," wrote centuries ago a wonderfully insightful Psalm which helps us understand the mind of God. He had a plan for us, and even wrote them down in a book! In Psalm 139 we read:

> *My frame was not hidden from you when I was made in the secret place. When I was woven together in the depths of the earth, your eyes saw my unformed body. All the days ordained for me were written in your book before one of them came to be.*
> *—Psalm 139:15,16 (NIV)*

Since God had this plan in mind, it is clear he is not sitting around heaven dreaming up ways to make our lives miserable. He doesn't put two people together ("set them") in order for them to lead frustrated and isolated lives. He intends them to understand their differences, and learn to value and appreciate them as he designed them! Eventually we see they actually work together for the greater good of the marriage, producing the desired takeaway from this chapter: *the fullness of what God has intended from the very beginning of time.* Marriages like this really ARE jewels set by the Master Jeweler! That is an awesome concept. God has always had each of us on his mind! He has "good stuff" waiting for us; we need simply to humble ourselves before God and our spouse, deny ourselves, and step into the fullness of joy found in his divine design.

Points To Ponder

So, is your spouse a barrier or a blessing in your marriage? Do you compete with each other or complete each other? Has the joy that was there in the beginning been wiped away, replaced by a mixture of monotony and moodiness?

Do you remember the movie *City Slickers*? The main character, unable to identify what has drained out of his life and marriage, is told by his wife to go away for two weeks on a cattle drive to "find his smile again." What would bring back that smile to your life and marriage? What would rekindle the passion?

The fact is, what you DO with differences makes a difference— one that will divide you or unite you. Lack of togetherness will affect how you feel about yourself as well as your mate. It will affect your children (they're watching, you know), your attitudes at work, your approach to money management, and the depth and quality of relationships with your friends. Why? Because God never planned for you to be alone— unity is his created order. If God led you to be married, only unity will produce the peace you long for, and banish any anger and bitterness that may bite away at the harmony of your soul and your spirit.

Genesis 2:24 says, "For this reason a man will leave his father and mother and be united (KJV "cleave") to his wife, and they will become one flesh." Notice the verbs: "leave," "cleave" and "become." On closer reading we can make these observations:

- ख़ Marriage is to be a *priority*
- ख़ Marriage is to be *permanent*
- ख़ Marriage is a *process*

Don't expect perfection overnight. Focus not only on the *destination*, but also on the *process*. Enjoy the ride. God created this thing called "matrimony" to be an enjoyable and fulfilling experience. After all, at one time there WAS some chemistry—some attraction and affinity—that drew you together. It's still there somewhere. It may be buried a bit, but it can be dusted off and pieced back together.

At the beginning of this chapter, we cited Ephesians 5:31. Paul further states in this passage, in verses 25-27:

> Husbands, love your wives, even as Christ also loved the Church and gave himself for it. That he might sanctify and cleanse it with the washing of water by the word, That he might present it to himself a glorious church, not having spot, or wrinkle, or any such thing; but that it should be holy and without blemish.
> —Ephesians 5:25-27 (KJV)

This is an absolutely beautiful picture. God says marriage is a reflection on earth of his Bride, the Church. He wants a pure, spotless bride. We'll sit down with him some day in eternity at a wedding feast. Meanwhile, he wants our marriages here on earth to be whole and wholesome—"washed" and made fresh—and he is able to provide the means to heal holes in our hearts and restore any wreckage that may have occurred along the way as a result of not paying attention to the danger signs. God offers his grace and blessing to wash the "junk" right out of marriages. As we have said, it requires great humility in order to reach this placid pool.

In an article in *Time* magazine, this not-so-great evaluation of marriage in America is made, in stark contrast to the picture painted for us by the Apostle Paul in Ephesians.

According to the research, married couples' assessment of the quality of their marriage starts to sink rapidly just after the "I do" and continues downward through the first four years. The quality of marriage plateaus after that first dip and then declines again during years eight, nine and 10 -- the "seven-year itch" part. Couples reported that the presence of children is, not surprisingly, a considerable stress on a marriage; the research states that having children at home prevented married couples from maintaining "positive illusions about their relationships."[1]

Time magazine

That's a bit like both our couples, isn't it? The "seven-year-itch." The Stuckeys have already experienced it and plateaued out as a part of their resignation to their situation. The Baileys are headed in that direction, too—fast! If they do not come to grips with their differences soon they will not even REACH the seven-year plateau.

You don't need to stay stuck like the Stuckeys! You don't need to bail out like the Baileys!

Here's a great scenario: you are actually looking forward to coming home. You're tired, and you have come to realize that your home is a refuge—a sanctuary of safety and security. You both need some time away from the noise level of life; it's been a demanding week. Over the past several weeks, you've been working hard on your relationship. You have both tried to watch your words—praising and not picking, protecting and not persecuting. Husbands, you have begun to compliment your bride more—after all, the Scriptures say you are to "rejoice in the wife of your youth" (Proverbs 5:18). Down deep you know you love her (she did make a really good choice in marrying you!), and, you're doing a better job expressing that to her. Wives, you are trying to affirm your husbands, seeking to become his "helper"—his "suitable helper." (Amazingly, he seems to be improving in his leadership in the home.) Hey! Maybe this unity thing works!

It's Friday night, the night you have chosen as a "date night"— the night you now devote to rebuilding what you once had—to "stoke the fire" again. There's a pilot light still burning down there somewhere (after all, God lit it!). Notice the flowers on the table. You've farmed out the kids (aren't you glad you have great friends?). The steaks are on the grill. The candles are lit. A little mood music is playing in the background. Can you smell those steaks cooking (or is that cologne)? Well… as the saying goes, you know the "rest of the story."

Chapter 3

The Problem With Problems

Rather, speaking the truth in love, we are to grow up in every way into him who is the head, into Christ, from whom the whole body, joined and held together by every joint with which it is equipped, when each part is working properly, makes the body grow so that it builds itself up in love.
—*Ephesians 4:15-16 (ESV)*

Dina Stuckey is excited. Like a child on Christmas morning, she has been looking forward to this Saturday. She has been planting seeds with Stu for weeks about looking at a new car to replace the one she has been driving for the past four years. She has dropped a number of trade-in hints, plus complaints about the battery and other malfunctions, thinking Stu will agree with her conclusion that replacing the car is the only *logical* solution.

Their daughters both have their usual weekend activities, so it will just be the two of them. Dina envisions a fun day of car shopping, lunch together at that new Japanese place—then stuffing that car in her shopping bag as if it were a new outfit at her favorite boutique in the mall! She has no idea what is *really* in store for her and Stu today.

She got up early—before Stu—and she's making him his favorite breakfast. The smell of freshly brewed coffee and bacon frying is wafting invitingly through the whole house. (She plans on buttering him up like one of those pancakes she is about to pour on the griddle— she wants this day to be perfect!) Dina had a hard time sleeping, but at the sound of the 6:30 alarm, her human dynamo mechanism engaged, and she suddenly became absolutely focused.

Dina has only one thing on her mind today: buying a car! Recently, without Stu's knowledge, she has been stopping by car dealerships after work looking at all the new models. She even has one picked out; now she simply has to make certain Stu will agree with her choice. She knows she will meet with some resistance, because the car she has in mind will clash with Stu's practical, utilitarian decision-making process. She wants a special car—a fun car—a red convertible! She's hopeful she can persuade Stu into spending the kind of money "her" car is going to cost.

She has polished and practiced her dialogue. Although this *should* be an issue she and Stu discuss together, their "discussions" often lead to misunderstandings or escalate into arguments— resulting in frustration for both of them. On one hand Dina does not want to act selfishly over this issue, but then she thinks, "After all, I contribute money to the family treasury, so I should be able to drive the kind of car I want. I work as hard as he does, and I'm the one who has to do all the extra driving—music lessons, soccer practice, women's meetings at church, and grocery shopping each week." She reasons that since Stu nixed the dream vacation cruise for next summer, they should have sufficient money to buy a new car—especially since they will be able to finance it over the next 60 months. That monthly payment should fit easily within their monthly budget.

In Dina's mind, today will be an exciting adventure. Since the Stuckeys have yet to learn how their different approaches to identifying and solving problems can benefit each other, the stage has been set for a different kind of experience than she imagines. You see, God has wired some of us to take a more aggressive approach to solving problems, while he has wired others with a more reflective approach. Conflict can arise when each of these two types of persons face off to solve a particular problem. Aggressive problem solvers take a step toward an issue, pick it up and start working at a solution. They meet it head on with boldness and confidence. Their problem solving approach is not better or worse—just *different*—from the approach taken by those who address problems reflectively.

Dina, the dynamic partner in the Stuckey household, is wired with an aggressive bent—she deals with issues head on. In the case of this car, she is exhibiting assertive behavior: she has what she "perceives" as a pressing problem that requires immediate action. She has taken her problem, packaged it, and is now treating it like a fire that must immediately be extinguished. It is *urgent!* It must be solved *now— today! In her mind, there is no way she is going to return home driving the same car she leaves in that morning!*

Enter Stu Stuckey—stage left. He vaguely remembers Dina getting up, but he was able to sleep a bit longer. Then he began to smell the coffee and bacon, and that roused him from the comfort of the covers. His bride didn't often cook a fancy breakfast on Saturday, so he was a bit suspicious. He got up, put on his robe and went downstairs to join his family. There awaiting him was his favorite breakfast—pancakes, bacon, eggs—the works. And freshly brewed *premium* blend coffee!

"Hey, Dad!" said his beautiful daughters. "Good morning," he said drowsily. Then, turning to Dina, he remarked, "What's up, honey?"

"Oh it's going to be a fun day! I have it all planned out. The girls are going over to their friend's house after their soccer practice this afternoon, so our day will be free after I drop them off for their music lessons this morning." Before Stu had a chance to say anything, Dina continued, "We are going to have a great lunch at that new Japanese restaurant right there on auto row—there are ten dealerships within two miles." (She is waiting for the perfect time to tell Stu that one dealership said they have a red convertible demo she could test drive until Monday.) Dina imagines they would go to dinner that evening at Fosters, their favorite restaurant, with the top down. "Stu will be so surprised," she is thinking, *but so will she!*

There was a method to her madness: she had a total *blueprint* laid out for them—a detailed plan. Interestingly, this degree of planning is something *Stu* would usually do, so she tried to match his methodology. Dina only went to these great lengths when it involved something *she* really wanted, and today she was *determined* to have her way!

Before Stu could even make an objection, she slid his plate of pancakes and eggs in front of him in an effort to distract him. (Stu knew from past experience this was not the time to say a word— he and Dina had been down this road many times before—and the outcome was not pleasant.) As Stu and Dina finished, their daughters left the table to get ready for their music lessons and soccer practice. That gave them a few minutes to continue their conversation. Let's listen in:

Stu: "I thought we were going to talk this over a little longer before we made a decision to replace your car. It's not *that* old and it only needs a few minor repairs. We can get a lot more miles out of it before we have to spend money on a new one. We are close to getting it paid off and I hate to get into a larger monthly payment.

I don't remember committing an entire *day* to running around with you just to *look!*

Dina: "Well, actually, we did talk. You may not remember it, but you said we could start looking, so I did. I know we cannot afford the top of the line, but I have a salesman who told me they would make us a killer deal on a demo they have in stock. If the cost were the same as one of the other "cheaper" cars why wouldn't we buy something that was superior? You *said* we should do some research before we replace my car, so I have been doing that, and I think I have found a really good deal. You did say we needed to analyze the issue didn't you?"

Stu: "Well, yes, but it seems as though you have already made a decision. I'm still putting some numbers in my spreadsheet on the computer to compare a new car payment against the current repairs your car needs, as well as ongoing maintenance costs. I really need to get a better handle on our total financial picture before we can make a knowledgeable decision about a purchase of this size."

Dina: "Stu, you *always* say that! I don't think we're talking about raising my car payment that much. Besides, you act as though the decision is all yours. I'm working too! I put money every month in the checking account, so I should have a say-so about how we spend it!"

Dina's selfish thinking has come to the surface and she is venting them through her caustic words, causing Stu to become hostile. At this point, we need a thermometer to measure the rising temperature!

Stu: "What do you mean you work too? That's not the issue. For your information, I did not agree to buy you a new car—I agreed that we could look and price cars to gather information to help us make the right decision to replace or repair the car. At work, we call this "due diligence." We don't need to rush into anything. We've got plenty of time. Its not like your car is leaving you stranded every day—it's a very good car. And now it's *your* money, not *our* money?

Why don't you just go look at cars by yourself; it doesn't look like you need me anyway, so I think I'll stay home.

Stu leaves Dina standing in the kitchen. Game over; headed for the showers. This is not working out the way Dina planned it at all!

Types of Problem Solvers

Aggressive problem solvers. Reflective problem solvers. By divine design, God, in his infinite wisdom, put one of each in this marriage. But Stu and Dina don't see it that way—they're "stuck" with their differences. They view their differences as annoyances— as barriers—to doing things the way they think they should be done! In this situation, which of them is right? Is one of them a winner while the other a loser? It depends on what lens you are looking through, or what standard you are using to gauge the situation.

In this instance, we know exactly who is aggressive and who is reflective. Do not mistake this as a gender issue. Rather, a single brain has initiated an action that could really make use of *two* brains! "Two heads are better than one," but two brains are not better unless they are of one mind. Dina has her purse in one hand and her car keys in the other; Stu is stewing and they haven't even gotten out of the driveway. There are no winners in this conversation—they are both losers from the standpoint of intimacy, closeness and unity.

Stu is the reflective problem solver. He is more peaceful, agreeable and cautious; he wants time to step away from the dilemma to reflect and size it up, assess and gather as much information as possible before beginning to solve it—he is "calculating." Dina—bold, competitive and strong willed—is "impulsive." When she sees a problem or challenge, she moves toward it, picks it up and begins immediately to solve it. Two different categories. Two different approaches.

Is there a solution to these divergent kinds of problem solving temperaments in marriage? Our premise in this book has been that it is easier to believe lies rather than truth. What is the truth about solving problems?

Consider this: every problem cannot be solved aggressively; in fact, many are *compounded* by this approach. Nor can every problem be solved reflectively; some problems *require* a sense of urgency. For Stu and Dina, this is a perfect illustration of how couples so often get "stuck" in their marriages, and how the problems can become more deeply entrenched the longer they are married. The Stuckeys don't *want* it to be that way! They are not adversaries! They love each other. *They just don't know what to do.* This is such a familiar road to them (as Yogi said, "It's déjà vu all over again!").

Again and again they have faced difficult decisions and attempted to solve them the best way they knew how, only to arrive at the same place: frustration, high blood pressure and further erosion of love and intimacy in their marriage.

Can you identify with this scene? Sometimes, spouses reverse the reflective or aggressive roles, but in each case the outcome is predictable. We have given our couple names in this story to protect the guilty—namely US!

Could it be that many of the conflicts in your marriage are associated not with the problems themselves, but with the way each of you approach *solving* the problems? Isn't it interesting that we often view our mate's strengths as weaknesses simply because how they approach difficult situations is different from our own?

Finding a Solution for the Stuckeys

In the case of the Stuckeys, the first step is to recognize that this is a decidedly emotional encounter. Somehow they must punch through the emotion of the moment to a higher level of objectivity; their mind/will/emotion mix is unbalanced. Stu moves from knowledge to will, while Dina's usual pattern is emotion to will. In this decision, Stu would not intentionally frustrate his wife by preventing the purchase of the car. And Dina would not force Stu to make an unnecessary expenditure if she truly understood all that was involved. Somewhere in the midst of this chaos, there is a balanced blend—an equitable solution—one that will make sense to both of them, and which will help, not harm their marriage or their financial position. They are a caring couple, and enjoy that sense of close communion they attain from time to time. Increasingly, they need to learn to slow down, pray and then plan, following the advice of Solomon, the wisest man in the Bible: "The heart of man plans his way, but the Lord establishes *(directs)* his steps" (Proverbs 16:9 ESV).

Another step is for them to understand that this reactive versus reflective approach to problem solving is not an *obstacle* but an *opportunity* to celebrate and affirm one another in the beauty of difference and the delicacy of divine design. We have established that differences are not the issue; it's what we *do* with that difference that really matters in marriage. Both Stu and Dina, as they approach this auto purchase, have insights to contribute to the process, and an important role to play in the drama. It is not a matter of strength versus weakness, or of success versus failure.

To help you see and better understand the strengths and limitations of people with natural, aggressive problem solving bents, as well as people who approach problems more reflectively, below are two important tables. These tables also include descriptions that depict how the strengths of each style, when taken to an extreme, can result in problems that may cause further conflict.[1]

Notice first, in Table 1, how accurately the dynamic qualities of Dina are described. Her strengths offset the potential limitations that Stu exhibits when approaching a complex problem or decision. Obviously, they could each draw on the strength of the other for balance. The potential sources of conflict have already been portrayed in this narrative: intimidation, defensiveness, close-mindedness, all of which are areas that will improve as Stu and Dina begin to work together more closely to dissolve their defensiveness.

AGGRESSIVE			
STRENGTHS			
Daring	Competitive	Forceful	Determined
Self-Starter	Tenacious	Forward-Looking	
POTENTIAL LIMITATIONS			
Impatient	Domineering	Blunt	Risk-taker
Strong-Willed	Egotistical	Desires Power	
POTENTIAL SOURCES OF CONFLICT WITH OTHERS			
	Intimidating	Confrontational	
	Close-Minded	Defensive	

Table 1

REFLECTIVE			
STRENGTHS			
Conservative	Low-Key	Careful	Prepared
Considerate	Vigilant	Self-Control	
POTENTIAL LIMITATIONS			
Avoids Conflict			Disagreeable
Slow Decision Making	Afraid		Passive
POTENTIAL SOURCES OF CONFLICT WITH OTHERS			
Obstacle to Progress	Close-Minded		Indecisive
Lack of Creativity	Refusing to Confront		Unmotivated

Table 2

Stu, the reflective partner, is pictured in Table 2. His sense of responsibility and vigilance lead him to act cautiously and carefully when making decisions. Dina will therefore help him to overcome his potential indecisiveness.

If Dina and Stu understood their personal problem solving strengths, laid out in the data in these tables, the private discussion we listened to might have played itself out quite differently. Dina loves to look, shop and decide—it brings her immense pleasure and she is quite proficient at it! When she sees what she wants she buys it, and it's over! Then she is off to something else. Stu, on the other hand, can be paralyzed in the decision making process, trying to make sure it is the "perfect" decision. Even after the decision has been made, he will need to reassure himself that it was the right one.

What if Stu, knowing how Dina solves problems, affirmed her in it? Further, what if he empowered her to benefit from the wisdom of solving a problem reflectively as well? His part would be to research consumer reports, compare models and identify those best suited to meet their needs. After all, he hates dealing with car salesmen! Dina could do the legwork, and come up with a few choice models—within their agreed upon price range—to show him, and save him the grief of driving all over town looking endlessly at car after car. Even thinking about that prospect makes his brain hurt.

Likewise, what if Dina reciprocally affirmed and validated her husband's strengths in corroborating data to determine the best makes and models available, as well as his years of skill in maintaining their family finances? His strengths will insure the purchase process will be researched completely, and that they are not being taken advantage of in terms of the sale price. Stu then will find himself complemented through Dina's abilities to segue with his own, just as she will his. His painstaking attention to detail is more important than the speed with which he makes a decision; this provides balance to Dina's impulsiveness.

You can see why Stu needs Dina, and why Dina needs Stu.

A New Look at the Problem

For this fresh approach to work, however, Dina must agree to curb her spontaneity and her tendency to lead a sales person into thinking she is there to buy immediately. And Stu needs to let go of his need to control, and include Dina, by communicating to her that he genuinely values her input. She is to "spy out the land" and bring back a good report, while Stu is to validate that information. When they set in motion this kind of partnership, Dina will begin to view her imagined *obstacles* as *opportunities*. Since she loves adventure, she is free to kick tires, smell the new paint and leather seats, while leaving the "boring" analysis of the data up to Stu.

Stu's forte is to manage the overall process in such a way that the best decision possible is arrived at for the family. He must spend enough time shopping with Dina to make her feel her opinions and needs have been fully taken into consideration. With this approach, each leads from their strengths. There is no "mine" versus "yours" vocabulary—only the sweeter sound of "ours"—a clue that their marriage is developing into a truly functional relationship. Not two living as two but two living as one.

After Dina has narrowed the field, and has three or four cars for Stu to look at (including that red convertible she *really* wants), they can then arrange for a fun day of test driving, lunch and time together, and then making the best deal.

Stu deals with the details at the dealership.

He makes certain that pricing, accessories, warranty, etc. are appropriate.

He researches thoroughly all the other minutiae: terms, best lending institutions, interest rates, maintenance history of the various brands, and so on. After all, complexities are his "stock in trade"—he is brilliant when it comes to managing intricacies. And Dina is the quintessential shopper! With their combined knowledge, wisdom and expertise, these two brains will be able to cook up something much better than a pancake breakfast! This complex decision, by combining the strengths of these two spouses, can be turned into a wonderful, harmonious symphony by simply reading from the same sheet of music.

So, let's rewind the tape: what difference would it make if Stu and Dina had a clearer understanding of their differences, and had begun to work at unifying their approach to buying this new vehicle? There would be quite a *different* conversation at their breakfast table on Saturday morning. This time, let's assume they have discovered this wonderful truth:

> *Two are better than one, because they have a good reward for their toil. For if they fall, one will lift up his fellow. But woe to him who is alone when he falls and has not another to lift him up!*
> *—Ecclesiastes 4:9-10 (ESV)*

Stu: "Good morning, ladies!" Turning to Dina, he remarks, "Wow! My favorite breakfast! The smell woke me up. Dina, you're the greatest. Are you trying to butter me up for something today?"

Dina: "No, honey. I just appreciate your willingness to go with me today to look at cars, so I wanted to do something special for you this morning. I thought it would be nice to drop the girls off for their music lessons so we can have the day just to ourselves."

Stu: "Well, I've finished the spreadsheets and looked at our savings. I think if we sell your car ourselves, rather than using it as a trade in, we will come out better than giving it to the dealership."

Dina: "You know I appreciate that about your dad, girls. He is always looking out for us. I must admit, Stu, that I have my eye on a beautiful new red convertible!"

Stu: "A convertible—in our agreed upon price range?"

Dina: "Yes! I found a demo and the salesperson said we could even drive it for the weekend if we wanted to. She said that might help us determine if a convertible is the right car for us, since we have never owned one."

Stu: "Watch those pancakes! I'm really hungry! My first thought is that a convertible doesn't seem practical."

Dina: "But I've always wanted a convertible, so can we at least *look* before you say no?"

Stu: "I'm sorry, Dina. I didn't mean to say we couldn't look. Thanks for the great breakfast. As soon as the girls are ready, let's hit the road."

When it comes to solving problems, are you the reflective or the aggressive partner? What impact would it have on your marriage if you embraced the concept of blending your differences to avoid problems when making decisions?

Coming to grips with reflectiveness/aggressiveness in a marriage relationship is important, but it is not merely a matter of understanding practical principles. We must also understand *God's* principles. We began this chapter with these verses:

> *Rather, speaking the truth in love, we are to grow up in every way into him who is the head, into Christ, from whom the whole body, joined and held together by every joint with which it is equipped, when each part is working properly, makes the body grow so that it builds itself up in love.*
> —*Ephesians 4:15-16 (ESV)*

Love in a marriage relationship is communicated in many ways, both verbal and non-verbal. Paul, in Ephesians 4, says we are to "build one another up." This is part of learning how to "work together properly." Verse 29 says our words are to benefit those who listen. Remember, Stu and Dina were not the only people around the breakfast table that morning. Their children were listening closely to the entire exchange of words, and gaining an education on how they might later interact with their mates. The Scriptures tell us that with our tongues we can bless one another, or curse one another.

In Proverbs, we read, "The tongue has the power of life and death" (Proverbs 18:21 NIV). We must all learn to speak life over our spouses, our children and our friends.

So, when facing a problem in your marriage, carefully guard your conversations. Remember that how your spouse solves problems may be different from your own, and that is a wonderful thing. Seek to value that! Their differing point of view should be seen as a way to complete you, not frustrate you.

Think about this: what kind of conversation will take place at *your* breakfast table the next time YOU are faced with the need to make a major decision?

Chapter 4

Do You See What I See?

Humble yourselves, therefore, under God's mighty hand, that he may lift you up in due time. Cast all your anxiety on him because he cares for you. Be self-controlled and alert. Your enemy the devil prowls around like a roaring lion looking for someone to devour.
—*1 Peter 5:6-8 (NIV)*

Summer is over, there is a chill in the air and the leaves will soon be changing color. *Are you ready for some football?* It's Monday night in the Bailey house and the weekly religious ritual is about to begin. Tiger is an avid sports enthusiast, and regularly follows his favorite teams. As usual, Kitty isn't looking forward to the season; she sometimes thinks football is more important to him than she is. Tonight, Tiger followed his usual routine: he picked up pizza on the way home from work, leaving Kitty to fend for herself. Now he's in the living room in front of his newly financed HD flat screen television, and Kitty is in the kitchen sifting through her pile of home magazines.

"It's going to be another one of those nights," Tiger thought, "but it's better than the face-off of last week." This weekly retreat into his own little world affords Tiger a few hours of respite—time he feels he has earned and which he deserves.

Last Monday night began with the usual pizza and football, but Kitty interrupted his TV time, wanting to talk again about her dreams of a home they could call their own. She was on one of her "talking sprees," and Tiger "listened," but he wasn't really listening. "Yes, dear," he nodded, all the while peeking over her shoulder at the march down the field of his team's rival opponent. The entire conversation had been repeated so many times it could have been recorded on his TIVO and simply replayed. A compressed version sounds something like this:

Tiger: "Do we have to talk about this again? I thought we put this to bed!"

Kitty: "Well, it seems as if you don't care—you never seem to do anything about my needs. Tiger, can't you understand how important it is to me to have a home of our own? We can't live in this apartment forever, and it's so hard to look for a house, knowing you aren't going to act on it!"

Tiger: "Kitty, we can't afford it right now, so why can't you try to see this from my point of view? When I'm ready, and I'm convinced it's the right time, then we'll do something."

Kitty: "You mean YOU will do something! When do I have a say in the matter?"

Tiger: "If I could trust you to pay the bills, you might realize what a tight spot we're in right now. Even with both our checks, I can hardly juggle things to make ends meet. If your school loans were out of the way we might be able to talk about a house."

Kitty: "That's really not fair. You're the one that insists always buy the best cars, the best clothes and live in this expensive apartment. It's not that I don't like it, but I would really rather be in a house of our own. Why is it that every time the subject of money comes up you have to bring up my college loans? I'm sick of your insinuation that my college debt is somehow worse than our other debt and that I am the primary cause of our financial turmoil. Remember YOU were the one that just had to get married before we graduated from college. It sounds like you think I am one of your "bad investments" and you wish you'd never married me.

"Look, Tiger, I hate arguing with you. I just think we need to talk these things over until we reach some kind of consensus. Instead, you just clam up and stop talking! We seem to have such divergent views when it comes to important issues."

Tiger: "Kitty, we're not getting anywhere with this. We always end up in the same place. I really want to watch this game. Can't you just read your magazines and keep dreaming for now?"

Here We Go Again

This has been a familiar thread in the fabric of the Bailey marriage, one that threatens to unravel the whole garment if this loose strand is not snipped! They have struggled with their differences since the "honey" from the honeymoon oozed out of their relationship. Tiger always takes the lead with his aggressive style when they have a pressing problem to solve—his determination has come through for them many times—and has helped Kitty realize how hesitant she sometimes is to make decisions. However, now she is perplexed— he has taken a back seat to their marriage and financial future and replaced his aggressiveness with passiveness and complacency.

Lately, because of the escalating level of conflict with Tiger, and the frustration she has been feeling—knowing somehow this is not the way marriage is supposed to work—Kitty has revived her old habit of journaling. Feeling she could not talk meaningfully with her husband, she needed an alternative means of sorting out her thoughts. Before she was married, she experienced great delight in maintaining her diary; only then she had focused on happier matters. Now, she has resorted to using it as a replacement for real communication with Tiger—a place to vent her frustrations. "Some kind of relationship" she thought; "I talk more to this book and to myself than I do to him!"

Tiger has come up with more and more reasons to be out during the week for work-related reasons, and now he and a group of his friends meet on Thursday night at Tim's house to watch more football on ESPN. Tim and Tiger are best friends and fraternity brothers; Tim earns twice what Tiger and Kitty make, and he has a lot of discretionary money—which only intensifies Tiger's jealousy. Tim got the house as part of his recent divorce settlement, and he just put in a new media room decked out with a huge screen and projection system complete with surround sound. The satellite hookup gives them access to unlimited sports, and Tiger doesn't usually get home on Thursday nights until past 11:00 pm. He says it is like being in college again.

He has also volunteered for several business trips lately that he could have delegated to someone else. His frequent absence avoids conflict with Kitty, but only intensifies her resentment toward him. What hurts her the most is that he has been excluding her from his innermost thoughts and feelings.

So, on this Monday night, rather than provoke another unpleasant altercation—she hates confrontation—Kitty decided to spend less time reading her magazines and invest more time reflecting on why their marriage seems to be on the brink of failure. "It probably doesn't help matters for me to be constantly looking at pictures and thinking about houses," she surmised. A favorite pastime of hers had become driving through new subdivisions, walking through model homes and dreaming about what it might be like to live in one of them. But the prices are absolutely scary! So tonight she determined to set aside distractions of all things pertaining to houses.

In addition to writing in her journal, she has also renewed her premarital custom of devotional reading. In high school and college she was fairly consistent in reading and praying, but married life and work began to dilute her priorities. As problems with Tiger mounted, she began to feel distanced, not only from him, but also from God. Slowly, her fervor faltered, and her spiritual life—prayer in particular—became nothing more than a prosaic pattern. If God could hear her, he didn't seem to be doing much about her pain—so she wondered why she should continue. Emotional energy began to drain out of her; it was as though her heart was shutting down, and as a result, she found herself lashing out at Tiger in an effort to make him feel the same level of pain she was experiencing! She knew this was wrong, but somehow his misery brought her pleasure.

At the beginning of their marriage, Kitty was quite optimistic, believing they would be able buy a home of their own in just a few years. She thought that was a mutual dream. Again and again she tried to convince Tiger they needed to get serious about saving for a down payment so they could have their own place, even if it was just a "starter home." Tiger knew the rent could be better spent toward making a house payment that built equity for them but he wouldn't settle for anything but the best. Trying to be persuasive, Kitty would talk passionately, but he would withdraw, which deflated her enthusiasm like letting the air out of a balloon. His inattention communicated to her that he didn't love her. Kitty believed Tiger was egotistically holding out for a big, showy place that would project to the world that he had arrived. She dreamed more about a comfortable cottage she could fix up and start a family. "Kids," she thought, "If we just had children, maybe Tiger would become more responsive toward me."

So here they were on another Monday night—Tiger and the TV; Kitty and her journal. "I guess it's better than no company at all," she reflected. She made this entry:

> _Dear Diary: He's in there watching football again. I tried to talk to him after we got home. He just ignored me and grabbed his pizza and headed for the TV. I think I have become invisible. I'm really getting tired of this! I don't know what to do. Maybe we really should think about separating and I should forget about having a house. What good would it do to buy one anyway? It wouldn't be a real home. I don't want to always nag at him, but he just won't listen to me. I know I've go to do something. God, I really need your help!_

Then she picked up her devotional book and began to read. Although she wasn't regular in her observance, she found some comfort and encouragement in the verses and the comments. A few days ago, Kitty read these words from the Bible, and had been pondering them ever since:

> _But godliness with contentment is great gain. For we brought nothing into the world, and we can take nothing out of it. But if we have food and clothing, we will be content with that._
> —1 Timothy 6:6-7 (NIV)

For the past several days, driving home from her office, she kept thinking about that word "contentment." She certainly had plenty of time to think: bumper-to-bumper traffic, four lanes and 20 miles per hour! If it weren't for the fact that she really enjoyed her job, plus the regular paycheck (their pre-marital plan was that most would go toward a down payment), it wouldn't be worth the hassle. Work seemed to be the only place she felt wanted, needed and accepted. "I wish that was how Tiger felt about me," she said to herself.

"Content?" she thought. She had noticed the words "food and clothing," but there was nothing said about housing—it was conspicuously absent! Surely that couldn't be. Everyone knows you have to have a house!

Can you identify with the Baileys? Is there a Monday night madness that might be crippling your relationship and draining energy and joy from your life? Does there seem to be no answer to the marriage and financial issues facing you? Are you seriously entertaining, even for a moment, the possibility of throwing in the towel? Don't stop reading now!

Optimistic or Realistic?

In any marriage, some are realists and some are optimists. In chapter 2 we painted a picture of the dangers of differences, and the difficulties of coming to grips with those differences. As we have said previously, God's plan for marriage is not to *frustrate* you with a mate who thinks differently than you, but to give you one that is a "suitable helper" to complement or *complete* you! *Blending differences is a crucial key to success within the fabric of marriage: the differences are like threads of different colors, and God is the Master Weaver, slowly but intricately interconnecting strands in order to create beautiful tapestries that reflect his own glory and creativity.*

In chapter 3, we saw that there are two approaches to solving problems: some people are aggressive and some are passive. Likewise, in our approach to handling people and information, there are two approaches: optimism and realism. The issue of "people and information" within a marriage revolves around whether we trust each other and the information we give one another, as well as how we seek to influence the other to accept our point of view. Do we rely on words and emotions to communicate, or do we use facts and data? Do we respond relationally or analytically?[1]

These two styles are very different, but both need to be understood if Kitty and Tiger are going to learn to communicate with one another effectively. This may be the key to salvaging the sagging underpinnings of their fragile home life. They are playing with matters larger than themselves—issues that could spell life or death for their marriage. The topic of the home purchase is just the current issue at hand, but the way this couple processes information is continually driving an invisible wedge between them. Kitty wants to mold Tiger to see things through her lens, causing Tiger to bolt with an even stronger resolve to do the same to her. They have spent the past four years of their married life trying to remake each other. Does this sound familiar?

As we did in chapter 3 we want you to examine the following tables, which list the strengths and potential limitations of the different styles of **processing relationships and information,** as well as the predictable areas of conflict that could arise when these styles clash.

Consider first those who approach people and information *optimistically.* They are expressive, outgoing individuals who possess innate persuasive abilities. They seem to trust people and information at a more surface level. They want to be trusted and they tend to trust others. Kitty is an optimist (table 1): she is

STRENGTHS

Optimistic	Inspiring	Friendly	Outgoing
Enthusiastic	Creative	Negotiates Conflict	

POTENTIAL LIMITATIONS

Trusts Indiscriminately	Lack of Discernment	Impulsive
Inattentive to Details	Overconfident	Unrealistic

POTENTIAL SOURCES OF CONFLICT WITH OTHERS

Unreliable	Overestimates Abilities	Friendly
Poor Listener	Unrestrained	Talks Too Much

Table 1

friendly, well liked by her colleagues at work, and by others in their apartment complex. She tends to build relationships quickly. One of her driving desires for a home is not only her "mother instincts" (she does want children in the future), but also her desire to express her creativity. However, she is over-optimistic, over-confident, and has not fully weighed the facts about their present financial position. Plus, she just plain *uses too many words to communicate with her husband!*

She accuses Tiger of being a poor listener; he actually is a good listener. She is simply not packaging her message in a way Tiger can receive it. Her many words are shrouded in emotion rather than logic, intensifying Tiger's inability to hear her. Kitty is the poor listener, and tends to focus on the next thing she is going to say before she has finished her present thought. Right now there seems to be no hope of achieving any degree of agreement, much less of learning to validate the strengths each possesses and the wonderful harmony they might experience if they truly "married" their respective strengths. If they were to physically separate, that would only confirm the mental and emotional separation that already exists.

Tiger, on the other hand is illustrated in table 2. He is a realist— factual, reflective and logical, at the expense of warmth and emotion.

Table 2

He validates everything—when new people or information enter the scene, he is critical. Tiger's trust must be earned, and it can easily be lost if the point of view lacks facts to support the information being presented. Thus, Kitty interprets this as a lack of love and concern. His piercing questions create an impenetrable barrier. Even in his dealings with colleagues, he is viewed as self-absorbed, unfriendly and pessimistic. Tiger has an aggressive bent as well, and when coupled with his need to focus on the facts, it can be a turn-off not only to his spouse, but also his friends and co-workers.

Toward a Turning Point

What do you think it would take to turn Tiger and Kitty around and point them in a direction that might produce effective communication? More money? How do you perceive they have arrived at this predictable, yet pointless position? Are their poor communication skills and inability to process information effectively creating the logjam that marks their messy marriage?

Interestingly, most often the attention-getter for us is *pain.* Pain is one of God's pathways that help produce significant changes in our lives. It is called by many different names: crushing circumstances, turning points, crises or "wilderness experiences." For each of us, it comes packaged differently, since we each are different—by divine design. The pattern is different, likewise the path, but the journey is similarly unpleasant. Oswald Chambers, in his well-known devotional book, *My Utmost For His Highest,* had incredible insights about God's pathway to change.

> God can never make us wine if we object to the fingers He uses to crush us with. If God would only use His own fingers, and make me broken bread and poured-out wine in a special way! But when He uses someone whom we dislike, or some set of circumstances to which we said we would never submit, and makes those the crushers, we object. We must never choose the scene of our own martyrdom. If ever we are going to be made into wine, we will have to be crushed; you cannot drink grapes. Grapes become wine only when they have been squeezed.[2]
>
> *My Utmost For His Highest*

The principle here is that God does not extend to us the privilege of choosing whom or what he will use to crush our grapes in the great winepress of life. God desires our constant, undivided attention in every area of life; when things seem to be deteriorating around us, it is often easier for him to get our attention.

For Tiger, this moment came during a performance review at work. He had expected a promotion, which carried with it a significantly increased compensation package. In his mind, that would have put him one more step up the ladder and closer to his perception of success. He wanted a home, too, as did Kitty. But his timetable was different, his plan was different and the style and location were definitely different. During the review, he was shocked into the reality that he was perceived by his superiors—as well as his colleagues and the three subordinates who reported to him— as insensitive, critical, cold, analytical to a fault, and a loner. He was informed that the company really needed team players.

Although he was not terminated, a warning was entered in his record and he was advised that he would be reviewed again in six months, with an expectation of improvement.

What an illustration of crisis!

Kitty's turning point was significant also—her performance review came from God through his Word! Remember the day she was struck by the issue of "contentment?" It continued. Day after day that word followed her like a shadow. Her conscience would not leave her alone. Let's peak at another entry she made in her diary (she won't mind):

Dear Diary: I think I am doing what I said I would never do—I have become a nag, just like Tiger's mom. It's no wonder he won't talk to me. It's like I can't ever say anything nice to him. He should be able to enjoy his well-earned Monday nights and time with his friends. He loves sports! I get to do MY thing, why can't he?

I think I'm selfish. That devotional about contentment is bugging me to death. I don't think I know anything about it. I'm not content. I don't think either of us is. We keep buying stuff we can't afford, I'm pushing him on the house, when I know as well as he does we can't afford it right now.

God, how do I make this right? Will you help me? I know I've got to tell Tiger. It will be so hard. I seem to talk a whole lot more than I listen. No wonder he doesn't respond! Maybe I should write him like I used to in college before we married—he always told me how much he liked it when I wrote.

What a set-up! These two spouses may finally be in a place to make a break-through in their relationship—that is, if they respond properly to their painful circumstances. It is not *mandatory* that you experience "pain" in order to find "gain" in God's economy: the Scriptures admonish us to simply, "...be doers of the word, and not hearers only, deceiving yourselves," (James 1:22). Through obedience, you may avoid some levels of unnecessary grief, but when you do not take heed to his commandments, God may chasten you because of his love for you (Hebrews 12:6). *Pain is designed by God to "make us better not bitter."*

Coming home the day of his performance review was a very long drive for Tiger. He had plenty of time to reflect on what his boss had said. It had really wounded him, but he began to accept the truth of the observations he had made, along with other comments from his co-workers. Either he would have to change, or he could bolt and head for some other company. However, he was honest enough with himself to acknowledge he would only be taking the problems with him. Something had happened to Tiger that hadn't happened before. The Bible calls this a "humbling experience." The opening verses of this chapter remind us to:

> *Humble yourselves, therefore, under God's mighty hand, that he may lift you up in due time. Cast all your anxiety on him because he cares for you. Be self-controlled and alert. Your enemy the devil prowls around like a roaring lion looking for someone to devour.*
>
> *—1 Peter 5:6-8 (NIV)*

Resolution and Reconciliation

Tiger dreaded having to face Kitty—she knew what was to happen that day, and she would ask him all about it. What a humiliating experience it was going to be! He began to realize as he was driving home that the same problems at work characterized the atmosphere of his home and his relationship with his wife. "What on earth am I doing?" he thought to himself. "I don't want to get fired from my job AND get fired from my marriage! That would be complete failure. I know I'm not a loser."

"Besides, she is a good woman. I remember the first time I saw her…" All of a sudden, the coldness began to melt, and his dread of the reunion gave way to hope for a better "union." As he drove up, he noticed Kitty's car in the driveway. He didn't know how this was going to turn out, but he hoped for the best. Let's listen in:

Tiger: "I suppose you want to hear about my review."

Kitty: "I'm sure you did fine. They probably told you again how they could not carry on without you and how they appreciate your contribution to the company."

Tiger: "Quite the contrary. I nearly got fired!"

Kitty: "What?"

Tiger: "Kitty, I have been doing some serious thinking. My boss had to tell me some really tough things that were difficult for him to say and just as hard for me to hear. But they were true. Basically I have been a jerk. "Sensitive" is not a word they use at the office to describe me, and I am sure you would agree with them. They told me I had many strengths, but I was blind to how I was responding to others. I couldn't help but think I have similar blind spots in our marriage. Today was a huge wake up call for me! I am afraid my career is falling apart and I feel the same thing is happening to us."

Kitty: "I can't believe I'm hearing this Tiger, and I so appreciate you telling me how you feel. I have been sensing the same thing about our marriage; however, I don't think our problems are entirely *your* fault—we are *both* messing up here. Look, we haven't been married that long, and no one has really helped us learn how to live as a married couple. Neither of our parents has modeled marriages we would like to reproduce and it seems like our friends are bailing out all around us. Just look at Tim and Lisa. I don't want to end up like either of our parents, or like Tim. I'm sure you don't either. I believe we need some help."

Tiger: "I think you're right about that, but where do we turn?

Kitty: "I don't really know.

Tiger: "I don't either, but I'm quite sure giving up on our marriage is NOT the answer. There *must* be something we can do. I know I'm ready, and I think you are, right?"

Kitty: "Yes, I am. God has been working on me—big time! And it seems like God has gotten your attention today through what happened at work—that had to have been very humbling for you. There is one issue I haven't really shared with you, Tiger, but I think God has brought it to my attention. I was reading a verse in the Bible the other day about "contentment." I have come to realize I'm not very content with what we already have, and I want that to change. Also, I have judged your lack of leadership in the house matter as your not loving me. I shouldn't be ragging on you and pushing you about buying a house, since you are the one that has a better handle on our financial situation. I'm really sorry."

Tiger: "I'm sorry, too, Kitty. Can you forgive me?"

The "Heart" of the Matter

All across America, there are countless couples just like the Baileys. They want to do something about the predicament they find themselves in, but they simply do not know where to begin. Maybe you are one of those couples. One of our objectives in the last two chapters has been to not only highlight practical principles for communication in marriage, but also to draw attention to applicable Biblical principles. In chapter 1 we stated four foundational presuppositions upon which we are basing this book, two of which apply to this section on communication and marriage:

>   It is impossible for you to truly love your spouse without the love of Christ

>   God created your spouse different from you to complete you, not defeat you.

It is also impossible to love your spouse without living in *obedience to God.* To do so means we must know what God requires. This information is conveyed to us in God's marriage manual, the Bible. This book should occupy a prominent place in your heart and in your home.

In this scenario, God has brought these two young people to an important crossroad in their relationship through the convergence of two issues: humility and contentment. Tiger was humbled through the experience of his performance review. Kitty was awakened through her devotional reading to her need of contentment. Relationally, they have each become acutely aware of their seeming incompatibility; they view things differently and they inaccurately communicate what they see to each other. Much of their financial condition can also be traced to this lack of interaction.

However, on a *spiritual* level—that dimension of life that cannot be overlooked—they have suddenly been shocked into a different kind of reality. Their new awareness of their character flaws—and God's action in their lives—has placed them in a position to choose obedience or disobedience to the truth God has revealed to them. Since God designed our spouses purposely to complement us, he may also use them as agents of change—to reveal areas of our lives that need the light of God's Word. Our mind-set should mirror that of King David when he penned these words:

> Search me, O God, and know my heart; test me and know my anxious thoughts. See if there is any offensive way in me, and lead me in the way everlasting.
> —Psalm 139:22-24 (NIV)

Differences produce God's desired result only if you accept them as his good and perfect plan. You must also live in obedience to God's command to love one another, despite those differences. *However, you cannot properly love your mate without receiving and sharing the love of Christ.* A house without God is not a real home, and it will always be subject to the winds of adversity that inexorably blow.

The issue, then, is not only whether you are an optimist or a realist, and how you learn to "optimize" your approach to coping with that dimension of your relationship with your spouse, but also how you react when God awakens your heart to something much deeper—to matters that matter most.

Chapter 5

Let's Talk About Change

We can make our plans, but the Lord determines our steps.
—*Proverbs 16:9 (NLT)*

The steps of a man are established by the LORD, and He delights in his way.
—*Psalm 37:23 (NASB)*

Friday dawned temperate and cloudless, and the Stuckey family, after their morning routine, has left for the day—Stu to his job as controller for a large manufacturing firm, and Dina to the travel agency for which she works. Their daughters ride in a carpool with their mother and two other junior high girls on her way downtown; another carpool mom drives them home in the afternoon.

This is the one day each week that Stu always looks forward to: not only because it is the end of the week, but because tonight is *family night*, the time set aside to be together, to connect with one another, play board games or watch movies. It is also OYO (on your own) food night. As is the case in his business, Stu likes predictable patterns in his family life, and the recurrence of this weekly routine is gratifying to him; in fact, he prefers planned activities rather than spontaneous ones. In his mind, this weekly family night establishes tradition for his children, and helps build character and commitment.

Dina likes family night for a different reason: she doesn't have to cook! And their daughters like it for an even different reason: they have an excuse to eat junk food! Dina and Stu initiated this practice a few years earlier as a discussion time to allow anyone in the family to clear the air, in an effort to maintain harmony in the home. Eventually, the evening grew into a fun time away from the television. Stu often read to his children when they were younger—books like *The Chronicles of Narnia* and *The Wizard of Oz*. It instilled a love of reading in the girls, which was one of their objectives.

As family night evolved, other components were added: now each week, one family member is extended the privilege of setting the agenda for the evening—this week it is to be board games. The food—tonight it was pizza and hamburgers—seemed to satisfy everyone. Stu loved to play games with his family, but seldom won. ("Who can compete with a teenager when it comes to games?" he thought.)

As they finished supper and the girls began to clean up so they could gather at the table to play, Stu retreated to the den for a quick look at the evening paper—first the business section, then the sports section. As he was reading, enjoying another cup of coffee and anticipating an enjoyable evening, he overheard Dina on the phone in the kitchen. The conversation caught his attention, so he ceased reading for a moment and listened intently to her end:

"Okay, I understand. And where shall we meet you? What time is dinner? Do we need to bring anything? Right. We'll be there. I'll call you in the morning from my office. What's that? Yes, Stu loves any kind of vegetable. When should we be there? Okay. We'll see you then."

Stu laid his paper aside and moved to the kitchen, where Dina was making notes on a note pad. "What was all that about? Who were you talking to?" he questioned.

"Oh, that was Jenny, (Dina's best friend). We are invited tomorrow night to her house with five other couples for a special dinner cooked by her nephew. He just graduated from a high-class culinary school. He's in town for one night and wants to do something special for her. It's going to be a great evening, and the best thing is I won't have to cook!"

"What do you mean tomorrow night? I already have plans! Don't you remember the basketball game I'm going to with Jim to watch his son play? It's a very important play-off game for him, and I made a commitment to go with them."

"Yes, I remember; but Stu, you go to his games all the time. I think this is more important—and something we can do *together!* I didn't think it would be too much to ask for you to change your plans. Don't you think doing things with *my* friends is just as important as with *yours*?"

"Dina, please don't do this to me—you know I don't like to break commitments! I don't care *how* important you think this is, you should have consulted me and given me some lead-time before expecting me to change my plans. I can't believe you do stuff like this! Now I don't even feel like playing our games. Why do you have to spoil our family night with one of your impulsive decisions that you've made without talking to me?"

Can you identify with this scene? Has this ever occurred in your home? This confrontation is not simply a matter of miscommunication between Dina and Stu. There exists something much deeper, both on a *practical* level and on a *spiritual* level.

In chapter 3, we followed the Stuckeys as they faced a different issue in their marriage: a decision regarding the purchase of a new vehicle. In approaching and solving problems, we said there are two kinds of people: aggressive or passive. Dina, as an aggressive spouse, was pressing Stu—her passive husband—to purchase a vehicle that had not been properly researched. Then, in chapter 4, we watched the Baileys struggle with the difference in how they process information. These contrasting types of communicators are referred to as either optimists or realists. Tiger, the realistic spouse in that chapter, was resisting his wife's optimistic approach toward buying a house; Kitty was insistent they move quickly in pursuit of securing a home.

Pace and Change

In this chapter we turn to another dimension of potential conflict: *pace* and *change*; that is, what kind of *environment* each spouse prefers, and how they react when faced with the prospect of making changes. God has wired some people to flourish in a *predictable* environment, while others prefer a *dynamic* environment. Within a marriage, these differences produce very predictable results! In the Scriptures, Job put it this way: "…man is born to trouble as the sparks fly upward…" (Job 5:7). Clashes produce such sparks! Why is this so? In the scenario with Stu and Dina, it revolves around this issue of pace and change within their home and their relationship (the following principles may also be applied beyond marriage and family to our jobs—how we relate to those with whom we work).

To summarize our progression, we have stressed up to this point several core values and principles:

1. God divinely designed our marriages, and he has given us unique mates for a unique purpose: to complete us, not defeat us.

2. We need to recognize and respect the God-given strengths of our mates and others around us—family members, co-workers and friends.

3. We need to learn to BLEND these differences to produce the intended harmonic whole God is seeking to produce in our lives and in our homes.

Blending involves bending—give and take—as loving marriage partners progressively come to understand the disparities that exist within their covenantal relationship. They prayerfully allow any adversarial attitudes they may harbor to dissolve as the light of God's Word gradually dispels the darkness of the lies they have believed. An overriding principle—above all those mentioned above—is that there is a *spiritual* dimension that affects our marriages, and we will never experience the depth of love our Creator intends for us until we are rightly related to him. Out of love for God a new depth of love for one another will emerge and strengthen our resolve to apply practical principles to even unidentified wounds that are deeply ensconced within us. The Scriptures admonish us:

> *Love from the center of who you are; don't fake it. Run for dear life from evil; hold on for dear life to good. Be good friends who love deeply; practice playing second fiddle.*
> —*Romans 12:9,10 (The Message)*

As we approach this new topic of pace and change, we invite you to examine the following tables, just as we have done in previous chapters. This time think about how you currently handle pace and change and what your strengths and limitations may be, as well as those of your spouse. The two tables also identify the sources of potential conflict that may occur when your mate exhibits a different preference style.[1]

Predictable partners (Table 1) in a marriage prefer a slower pace, so they usually resist change. It is not that they resist it simply for the sake of resistance; they resist it because they do not understand how it will impact their plans. Predictable people are planners, and they are finishers. They may not start many projects, but everything they start, they finish! Because they are planners, they have schedules and plans labeled, "do not disturb."

P R E D I C T A B L E	STRENGTHS		
	Good Team Player Stable Under Pressure Patient Finishes Tasks Great Listener		Logical Methodical
	POTENTIAL LIMITATIONS		
	Slow Paced	Inflexible	Controlling
	POTENTIAL SOURCES OF CONFLICT WITH OTHERS		
	Lacks Sense of Urgency Stubborn Apathetic	Avoids Confrontation Actively Resists Change Possessive of Information	

Table 1

Those with this temperamental quality are valuable within a marriage, on the job or in other positions of responsibility outside the home, because of their *natural desire to serve*. Helping others actually *energizes* them. They are generally methodical, patient and stable. They exhibit high levels of loyalty—important in marriage and team situations—though with fewer people than those with a dynamic bent.

The limitations of predictable people are also described in this table: mainly their inflexibility and their desire to maintain control of their environment. Inflexibility is sometimes perceived as stubbornness and apathy by a spouse or co-worker. Predictable people actively avoid confrontation! They rarely delegate, preferring to place one foot in front of the other at their own pace, insuring the timely completion of every project for which they are responsible. They may be viewed as lacking a sense of urgency, anathema to the dynamic partner in a marriage!

Predictable people follow this maxim: "ready, set, STOP! We must plan before we GO."

Dynamic people, by contrast, (Table 2) tend to prefer fast-paced environments that reflect variety and high energy. They are like jugglers, with many balls in the air. They are able to manage many projects at once, even though they complete few. We often refer to these people as "multitaskers," like computers with dual or quad processors! They are highly visible and involved, strenuously acting as change agents, often irritating those who do not particularly desire nor enjoy change.

D Y N A M I C	STRENGTHS			
	Energetic	Dynamic	Spontaneous	Flexible
	Involved	Versatile	Progressive	
	POTENTIAL LIMITATIONS			
	Impatient	Intense	Impulsive	
	Irresponsible	Restless	Hurried	
	POTENTIAL SOURCES OF CONFLICT WITH OTHERS			
	Unorganized	Everything is a Priority	Insensitive	
	Lacks Follow-Through	Change for Change's Sake		

Table 2

They are emotional and expressive—dramatic we might say—intensely focused on achieving a desired end. Predictable people may perceive the behavior of dynamic people as impulsive, frenetic or hurried—having no particular end in mind. While those with predictable patterns are alleged to resist change for the sake of resistance, dynamic people supposedly crave change simply for the sake of change! Dynamic people are thus labeled as unpredictable, in stark contrast to those who are highly predictable.

Taken to an extreme, those who demonstrate dynamism may make decisions impulsively or irresponsibly, insensitive to a marriage partner, a superior, a teammate or co-worker. Potentially the conflicts that might ensue with predictable people revolve around their recognition of dynamic behavior: lack of follow-through, lack of organization or spurious treatment of every project or decision as a priority, when in fact it may not be. The dynamic person plans—he just plans differently.

The motto of a dynamic person is, "ready, set, GO! We can plan along the way!"

Responding to Change

Starters. Finishers. Predictable. Dynamic. It is obvious here that both approaches are valid and necessary in marriages, as well as in other settings. And it is apparent in the Stuckeys which is the *predictable* partner, and which is the *dynamic* partner. Change is difficult for most of us, due to temperamental differences, gifts and callings, and the affects of aging. Once again, we appeal to the reader to grapple with the issue of understanding differences—here with regard to environment and change—and the need to blend the strengths of each, in order to achieve the balance that is needed in our marriage, job, church and family.

Since you are flanked on every side with different types of problem solvers, informational processors and change agents, it is important for you to begin to recognize your own tendencies and submit to the searchlight of truth that may be shining upon your life.

Thoughtfully consider what kind of environment you prefer and how you react to change. Are you predictable or dynamic? And are you actively seeking to blend your strength with that of your mate? Or are you even AWARE of your differences in this arena? Remember it is what you *do* with difference that will unite you or divide you!

Overcoming Limitations

So...here are the Stuckeys—stuck again! Dina has overwhelmed her husband. As a predictable person, Stu had a plan, and was working his plan. Dina *assumed* or *presumed* that she knew what was best for that given situation. Stu perceived her action as controlling and insensitive—perhaps even disrespectful of his authority in the home. Armed with little knowledge and information, Dina, true to her dynamic nature, on the spur of the moment made a decision without consulting her spouse. Stu once again "stewed," and reacted predictably, in total disagreement with Dina's sense of urgency, feeling on an emotional level that she had encroached upon his plans. In his mind, he now had to choose between disappointing his wife or breaking his commitment and thereby disappointing his friend. In his mind, it is a no-win situation.

Let's perform some reconstructive surgery on the little drama we have witnessed. Remember, Dina has strengths, as does Stu. They simply need to fit them together, or *mesh* them, in order to produce a better outcome. Dina is spontaneous; Stu is predictable. She is outgoing, and can easily open conversations; he is quiet and reserved. So, if these two learned to work in concert, the conversation might have sounded more like this:

Dina (on the phone in the kitchen): "Oh, hi Jenny. No, I have not mentioned tomorrow night to Stu. Let me see if I can talk to him right now—can I call you back?"

Stu (from the den): "Who was that, honey?"

Dina: "It was Jenny. Can we talk for a moment, or would you prefer to wait until you finish the paper?"

Stu: "Now is fine. What's up?"

Dina: "Jenny's nephew, who just graduated from culinary school, is in town for one night, and she is inviting several couples over for dinner for him to show off his skills as a way of encouraging him."

Stu: "Have you forgotten I have plans to go to the basketball game with Jim and his son? I can't just break a promise without at least consulting him."

Dina: "Well, you have been to several of his games already this year and this won't be the last game of the season. This is her nephew's only night in town."

Stu: "I still think I need to keep my commitment to Jim. Here's an idea: why don't you talk to Jenny and see if you can go to the dinner alone; I'll stop by after the game and join you for dessert."

Dina: "That sounds like a good plan, Stu. Let me call her back and see if that will work. I really appreciate your flexibility."

God's View of Planning

Remember this truth: there are consequences that derive from our actions. One area involves our commitments. Making commitments is highly important to God. Through Solomon, he makes this pronouncement:

> When you vow a vow to God, do not delay paying it, for he has no pleasure in fools. Pay what you vow. It is better that you should not vow than that you should vow and not pay. Let not your mouth lead you into sin, and do not say before the messenger that it was a mistake.
> —Ecclesiastes 6:4-6 (ESV)

A commitment is a type of vow. Stu made a commitment to his friend, Jim, and wisely, he was unwillingly to break it. In our culture, we have become flippant about our commitments, always keeping our options open. We like the word "maybe"—we don't want to say "for sure" because something *better* might come along! This rationale is at the heart of decisions that may lead to divorce in our society. If there is no sense of commitment in a relationship—no real *covenant*—men and women feel the freedom to dissolve that relationship because of "irreconcilable differences." Could these be the differences we have been discussing in this book? Is divorce the answer when one wakes up and finds that their spouse thinks differently and handles problems differently than they do? What constitutes an irreconcilable difference? Is it simply a selfish desire?

You may think it odd to put a calendar item (Stu's commitment to a basketball game) in the same category as divorce. However, stop to think about this: if you speak to someone, and commit to him or her that you will do something or be somewhere, and then you break that pledge, you have broken a vow—you have uttered a lie. The shattered promise is not only counted as a lie in the context of your relationship with the offended party, but as a broken vow before God himself! In other translations, the Ecclesiastes passage says, "…When you vow a vow BEFORE God…" In other words, when you make promises or vows, you do so in the audience of Royalty!

How do *you* view vows? Are you concerned about your commitments? Do you proffer   promises that you do not fulfill? The New Testament has this to say about the matter of commitments, referring to them as an "oaths":

> But above all, my brothers, do not swear, either by
> heaven or by earth or by any other oath, but let your
> "yes" be yes and your "no" be no, so that you may not fall
> under condemnation.
> —James 5:12 (ESV)

In Dina's case, perhaps without knowing it, she expected Stu to violate his vow. Stu's strength could have complemented her potential limitation because he is a prolific planner. She needs to learn to value and *compliment* that strength in him, and see it as a means of *complementing* her; then she will begin to see the multiplied strength of their good-becoming-great relationship.

As a point of clarification, there is one kind of commitment that does not necessarily constitute a vow. The Scriptures say we are wise to make plans, but we also must allow God the right to override them:

> *We can make our plans, but the Lord determines our steps.*
> —Proverbs 16:9 (NLT)

Here, note the words, "*our* plans." This type of plan does not necessarily reflect commitments that you make to others. These are matters that pass between you and God, and, if they involve your spouse, they should definitely be discussed in concert. Ask yourself: Do I allow God to direct my steps? To haphazardly aim at nothing by allowing life to simply "happen" will only ensure you hit nothing or achieve little. God instructs us to do things in a "fitting and orderly way" (1 Corinthians 14:40 NIV).

Stu and Dina have established a fine tradition: family night is a practical pattern for communication between family members, and for deepening relationships. But they are by no means "home free." They still exhibit many of the flaws described in Tables 1 and 2. It may take them some time to make major improvements in harmonizing their differences. Hopefully, the Stuckeys may provide a snapshot for you of where you might be at this moment in your marriage. That is a first step toward improvement.

You may want to consider instituting a *family night* in your home if you do not have one—it will broaden your understanding of one another, spouses as well as children. It will also provide a safe place to air grievances, and an unstructured time to "let your hair down." It's also just plain fun!

As a further suggestion, think about setting another precedent for keeping your marriage alive: a regular *date night*. The purpose of this evening, which might take place as frequently as weekly, but no less than monthly, is to fill in the communication gaps that subtly creep into a marriage, to compare and synchronize calendars, to keep the air clear and above all, to pray and to do everything necessary to ensure that the LORD is directing your steps! It too, might even be fun!

As a resource, we recommend you investigate this idea further through David and Claudia Arp's excellent book, *10 Great Dates to Energize Your Marriage.*[2]

As you begin to further understand your differences with respect to change, ponder this promise from God's word as you labor diligently to blend your predictable and dynamic strengths keep Proverbs 16:3 in mind—"Commit your work to the LORD, and **your plans will be established**."

Chapter 6

Who Needs Rules?

*Now faith is the substance of things hoped for, the evidence
of things not seen.*
—*Hebrews 11:1 (KJV)*

Set your affection on things above, not on things on the earth.
—*Colossians 3:2 (KVJ)*

Everyone has dreams. It is said that dreams are the "stuff that life is made of." Most people pursue passions. Dreams and passions fashion our hopes. Solomon, one of history's wisest men, said, "hope deferred makes the heart sick, but a desire fulfilled is a tree of life" (Proverbs 13:11 ESV). Hope produces motivation and derives from our purpose in life. Our purpose is framed by our worldview, from which flows our value system. Life's choices are made on the basis of our value system.

Tiger Bailey has been dreaming. And he has been pursuing his passions—sometimes subtly and sometimes aggressively. Many times his aggressiveness has gotten him into trouble. But today things seem to have taken a turn for the better! "Perhaps," he thought, "I've finally turned a corner."

He was daydreaming again as he merged into the busy commuting traffic that surrounded the city like so many ants crawling over an anthill. Yes, he had dreams…and hopes. He began to smile as he replayed a scenario wherein which he and Kitty were finally out of debt. As the picture was brushed on the canvas of his mind, he could almost experience the reality of the scene and how he would feel on that special day.

As he merged into the fast lane, he was quite pleased with himself. After all, he had worked very hard for nearly a year to restore his reputation following his "near miss" encounter with his boss, which had resulted in the last poor performance review. But his career was back on track. Actually, he had come to enjoy the spirit of team playing that he had not exhibited when he was first hired into his firm.

Now he had been rewarded! Justly so, he thought. A new office and a raise—a significant one and since it was the result of his labor he felt he should have the right to dictate where the money would be spent. His raise was not enough to say his ship had come in but you could at least see it on the horizon.

Tiger had called Kitty at work and told her to meet him at their favorite restaurant for dinner. This was the very place he had asked Kitty to marry him, and he thought it an ideal environment to "break the good news." He began to map out in his mind the strategy he would use to convince Kitty concerning the use of the increased revenue in the Bailey treasury. He was so confident of himself, and so filled with anticipation that he didn't even mind the grueling slow pace at which the traffic was moving. All he could think about was how quickly he could get out of debt. "I think I can finally get us on track financially and pay down some debt," he thought. It never crossed his mind what was about to happen to his special day and how differently Kitty might choose to spend the extra money.

Kitty was driving, too. She had left her office early in order to meet Tiger. Puzzled by his phone call, she could not help wondering what was going on. Why would he ask her to come to the restaurant on a Thursday night? She loved this place, since it did bring back memories of romance. But this was Tiger's usual boy's night out (and the night she had come to enjoy being alone). Knowing Tiger so well, she suspected that "something was up," that this was to be more than a romantic interlude on the lake .

Over the past several months, Kitty had continued her devotional reading and journaling, and her faith was growing. She and Tiger had attended church more regularly, but he still didn't seem to engage as much as she. Uncertain as to the purpose of this meeting, Kitty began to pray as she drove: "Lord, please help this to be a really good night with Tiger."

So, picture this: Tiger and Kitty speeding toward another intersection in their lives—a possible collision—a crossroads that could cause another strain on their still fragile marriage. Tigers raise is about to raise the roof.

Blending and Bending

To reiterate a concept from chapter two: we need a sign posted at the doorway of our hearts when interacting with our spouses: *"danger, differences ahead."* Throughout these pages, we have aggressively addressed the issue of differences: the dangers when dismissed and the benefits when blended. We have noted that in most marriages some are passive and some aggressive. We have also seen that some are realists, while others are optimists. In chapter 4, we identified Tiger as a realist and Kitty an optimist. Her optimism, however, is faltering at the moment. She took a deep breath and turned in to the restaurant, glancing around for Tiger's car in the lot.

Tiger arrived first. He had made reservations, and was already seated. Smiling as she entered, he greeted Kitty with a kiss on the cheek and seated her.

As we have previously done, let's tune the dial and listen in on the Bailey conversation:

Tiger: "Hi, honey. How was traffic? Did you have a good day?"

Kitty: "Traffic was awful as usual, but my day was pretty uneventful. What's going on?"

Tiger: "What do you mean?"

Kitty: "Well, I know something pretty big must be on your mind for you to give up Thursday night with the guys for me. After all this is my favorite place, and it's certainly better than eating by myself, so I'm not complaining. Besides, I get to be alone with you."

Tiger: "Yeah, kind of brings back memories, doesn't it? Let's order and then I'll fill you in."

Quietly, they each order. It's early, so the dining room isn't crowded. Music is playing softly in the background, setting a relaxing mood. They both need some time to wind down from the pressures of the day. Each of them waits to see who will break the silence.

Kitty: "Tiger, is something wrong?"

Tiger: "On the contrary. You remember how I got that last poor performance review? Well, I have been working pretty hard to repair my reputation. My last review was a huge wake up call and really helped me begin to make some needed changes. This past one I got a very high assessment. And all those extra hours of work at the office have finally paid off! I got a really large raise beginning next pay period! And, on top of that, they assigned me that office I have had my eye on."

Kitty: "That's great! I'm so happy for you, Tiger. Does that mean we will finally be able to look seriously at houses?"

Tiger: "Now wait a minute—slow down! I am not sure we can just go get a house hunting just yet but I have some ideas. I have thought of some things that will help us financially."

Kitty was quiet for a moment, as she remembered what she had prayed on the way there. She chose her words carefully, in order to avoid conflict. "Like what? I thought we agreed that when our financial status changed you would make the house a priority."

Tiger: "Well, I think we need to be cautious here. We need to do some planning and thinking before we just jump into something like a large mortgage. I know we have discussed it, but I'm still not sure it's the right time."

Kitty: "But we're not talking about a huge mortgage, remember? You're the one that wants to hold out for the big, fancy house. This seems like the perfect time for us to get out of the apartment and quit paying rent. You talk about money and budgets all day long at work, but when it comes to our finances, you seem paralyzed. You are so indecisive and analytical it kills me."

"What sort of big plans do you have, anyway?

Tiger: "Kitty, we've discussed the need to eliminate your school loans and all the credit card debt we've accumulated. What makes you think we can push ahead right now on such a big decision and a long term commitment like a house?"

Kitty: "But it seems to me that this raise should help reduce some of your financial concerns. I'm willing to take the plunge on owning our own home. Although our payments will be higher, at least we will be building equity for us, not someone else. Anyway, what do we have to lose? Don't you think it's worth a try? Why is that so scary to you?"

Tiger wants to go slow, Kitty wants to jump now. They have been at this place many times before. Tiger and Kitty have reached a familiar address: "stop; do not pass go; do not collect 200 dollars."

Tiger thought to himself. "I know she is serious about wanting a house, but I always feel like I'm being challenged and manipulated. She always wants to push the envelope."

He had wanted to share his plan for step-by-step systematic reduction and total elimination of their current debt, which would only take 4 years and 2 months considering his raise. His thought was that he got the raise so he would be the one to decide how the money would be spent. Wrong!

Before the salad was brought to the table he had learned he was going to have a hard time selling his idea.

Rules of the Road

Within a marriage, spouses relate to rules and boundaries differently: some are willing to take risks while others are more cautious. This variance has a profound impact on the growth and development of a marriage. Embracing dissimilarities in this area will enhance decision-making and better foster the blending of the strengths of each.

In every marriage, God has wired some to be structured and some more pioneering. Examine the following tables, and determine the strengths you bring to the relationship as well as the strengths your spouse brings to the table in light of of the need or lack of need for structure. Some people desire to follow rules and procedures, and some seem to make up their own as they go. When these two styles collide, conflict is inevitable.

Table 1 lists strengths, and potential sources of conflict for those with the structured style. Tiger, with his need for structure, has to "color within the lines," while Kitty doesn't mind coloring right up to the line. In fact, if she strays outside the boundaries, she might tell you why the line shouldn't be there in the first place! "Potential Sources of Conflict With Others" lists some of the ways that this conflict might manifest itself.

Study Table 1 with an eye toward application. Try to place yourself in one or the other category. Understanding these two styles in relation to rules and procedures could vastly improve your own situation in your family or on your job.[2]

S T R U C T U R E D	STRENGTHS		
	Conscientious	High Standards	Fact-finder
	Analytical	Conservative	Cautious
	POTENTIAL LIMITATIONS		
	Slow Decision Maker	Exacting	Perfectionist
	Overanalyzes	Oppressive	
	POTENTIAL SOURCES OF CONFLICT WITH OTHERS		
	Indecisive	Close-Minded	Unyielding
	Causes Gridlock	Critical	Distrusting

Table 1

People with a structured style tend to follow established rules and procedures in all areas of their lives. They are conscientious people with high standards, and highly honed analytical skills. They believe there is only one correct way to do anything. If they question any procedure, they passionately pursue the "right way" because they are precise, exacting and detailed. When they encounter obstacles, they freeze.

If you want to influence them, you had better have a lot of data and proof. They are not swayed by emotion, or with an abundance of words. Kitty's emotional cry for a home was not being heard by Tiger. Tiger is persuaded by sound analytical data or reasonable proof before he can feel confident to proceed in any direction. Kitty's desire to move is an obstacle in Tiger's eyes. She talks but Tiger is unable to hear her. The emotion of the moment—Kitty's strong desire to get her point across—fails to break the barrier between them.

The structured person has different potential limitations: over-analysis, slow decision-making and perfectionism, to name a few. This can lead to indecisiveness and a critical spirit. It is easy to project their high standards on others, resulting in appearing as obstinate and unyielding. In a marriage, spouses may view this person as unable to take advantage of opportunities immediately before them (Kitty's view of the raise).

In Table 2, note that the strengths of the pioneering person, not surprisingly, revolve around their ability to think "outside the box." They are usually visionary, and not bound by the status quo. They think there are better ways to do things, and they are willing to be bold enough to take the risks necessary to achieve goals. This may even involve bending or breaking established rules or protocols. They believe doing something is better than doing nothing. When they encounter an obstacle, they remove it or go around it.

P	**STRENGTHS**		
I	Self-Reliant	Decisive	Questions Status Quo
O	Independent	Bold	Risk-Taker
N	**POTENTIAL LIMITATIONS**		
E			
E	Ignores Consequences	Impatient	Out of Control
R	Insensitive	Controversial	Unorganized
I	**POTENTIAL SOURCES OF CONFLICT WITH OTHERS**		
N			
G	Reckless	Overconfident	Indifferent
	Overlooks Details	Haphazard	

Table 2

This pioneering style can lead others to view them as insensitive to the feelings of other people, or even out of control or controversial. They irritate structured people, who like to maintain their straight-line thinking, even if their strong personalities push against their counterparts. In reaction, those with pioneering tendencies push the other direction, exacerbating and escalating the issues at hand. The cautious, structured person within a marriage may view a pioneering spouse as reckless or haphazard, even though in the mind of the pioneering spouse, they are confident they will find a way to reach their goal.

But the real question is: are they *shared* goals?

Hopes and Dreams

Kitty and Tiger both have dreams. They both have hopes. They both have goals and passions. They have value systems, a worldview and sources of motivation—the whole mixture of what makes us human and alive. Hope is incredibly important; in fact, the Bible calls it the "anchor of the soul." Without hope we atrophy in spirit, soul and body.

But there is a difference between what we hope FOR and what we hope IN.

Misplaced, or misguided hope results in frustration when focused on material or temporal things. Paul's admonition to the young pastor, Timothy, was:

> *As for the rich in this present age, charge them not to be haughty, or to set their hopes on the uncertainty of riches, but on God, who richly provides us with everything to enjoy.*
> *—1 Timothy 6:17 (ESV)*

Notice: material things (riches) are uncertain. And, we are not to place our hope or our trust in them, but rather in God. Properly focused hope removes the barrier of always "hoping FOR the next great gift or goody." Things don't satisfy. Only God does!

The Psalmist understood this when he uttered these words to his own soul (have you ever spoken to your soul?):

Why are you downcast, O my soul? Why so disturbed within me? Put your hope in God, for I will yet praise him...
—Psalm 42:5 (ESV)

Once again, we are admonished to place our hope (our desires, our affections, our longings) on God, and not things. But on balance, the Timothy passage also reminds us that God GIVES us gifts richly to enjoy! They simply must not be our focus. Hoping FOR something could take many forms:

- I hope I won't stay single all my life
- I hope I get a raise this year
- I hope I get a nice gift for Christmas
- I hope I can get a nice house to live in
- I hope I can buy a sailboat some day

God dealt with Kitty once before on the critical issue of her lack of contentment. She seems to have forgotten.

God dealt with Tiger on the issue of humility in his aggressive leadership style in his job (and his marriage). He, too, has digressed and seems to have almost come full circle with his "I'm Back!" attitude.

Calming the Storm

People may think there is no glue to mend broken promises and relationships, but we don't accept that. Woven into our story of the Baileys is the glue of grace—the gospel of forgiveness. Coupled with the information, tools and techniques presented in these chapters, restoration can weld wounds and heal hurts for Kitty and Tiger.

In the midst of massive misunderstandings, truth has lost its traction for them. This couple represents an "island of reason in a sea of passion." Their structured vs. pioneering styles have clashed, fueling again in their subconscious minds the possibility of divorce.

As followers of Christ (albeit immature), this concept ought to be void from their vocabulary. But, their human frailty wants an out.

What they need, of course, is an environment of encouragement. In the beginning of this century, we continue to suffer from a dizziness of activity and a lack of peace. T.S. Eliot made this observation in his poem *The Rock*.

Eliot contends man has substituted 'gods' for God, and in our culture, it seems we worship money and possessions as god. Kitty's dogged determination to defend her position at all costs, an obvious obsession, has slowly but surely driven a widening wedge between Tiger and herself. But beyond this financial barrier, they have another perplexing problem.

> The endless cycle of idea and action, Endless invention, endless experiment, Brings knowledge of motion, but not stillness; Knowledge of speech, but not of silence; Knowledge of words, and ignorance of the Word. All our knowledge brings us nearer to our ignorance, All our ignorance brings us nearer to death, But nearness to death no nearer to GOD. Where is the Life we have lost in knowledge? Where is the knowledge we have lost in information? The cycles of Heaven in twenty centuries Bring us farther from GOD and nearer to the Dust.3
>
> *The Rock*

Tiger and Kitty have never learned to effectively communicate, a common source of clogging within the mechanism of marriages. There is within the human spirit a perverse disinclination to work in a harness with one another! Learning to work together requires non-corrosive communication between two people who increasingly enjoy the surrounding presence of the love of God. This young couple, like many of us, needs to awaken to the realization that we are fashioned for faith!

We have referred previously to the Book of Ephesians. The Apostle Paul has this to say: "Do not let any unwholesome talk come out of your mouths, but only what is helpful for building others up according to their needs, that it may benefit those who listen. And do not grieve the Holy Spirit of God, with whom you were sealed for the day of redemption. Get rid of all bitterness, rage and anger, brawling and slander, along with every form of malice" (Ephesians 4:29-31 NIV). We find here solid instruction on how to control our tongues and sanctify our conversations.

The confrontational interchange we were privy to might have been avoided had Kitty and Tiger realized from their last encounter how very different they are in nearly every area, and how very differently they approach life's issues. They differ in optimism vs. realism; and now with relationship to how they approach structure within the boundaries of their marriage.

After sharing the good news of his raise, Kitty, understanding Tiger's realism and his need for structure and order, ought to have known that he would have carefully crafted a plan as to the use of the increased income. She might have encouraged him to show her his ideas, demonstrating her trust in his leadership. Having worked and previously prayed through her lack of contentment, she should realize that God is in control of their lives and their finances, and that he wishes to maintain his role as Provider.

Tiger, on the other hand, rather than being defensive, ought to have immediately assured his bride that he had devised a plan that would assure her of a specific time—a realistic goal—toward which they could plan and work for fulfillment of her desire for a home.

Kitty has only seen Tiger as an aggressive businessman trying to make his mark on the world; she has not recognized the subtle changes that have occurred over time as the demands of his profession have polished the edges of his personality.

The mellow music, the evening away from their usual pursuits and the desire for moral dialog, provide an ideal setting to ignite the euphoric spark of possibility for them both. First of all, the spiritual dimension of their marriage must be cultivated more diligently, but they have practical matters to attend to as well. They need a better understanding of the decisions and practices that led them into financial disarray in the first place. And that is precisely why we will further pursue those matters in Part II of this book.

It seems the Good Ship Bailey may have smoother sailing ahead!

Chapter 7

The Mystery of Differences

*"For this reason a man will leave his father and mother and be united to his wife, and the two will become one flesh. **This is a profound mystery**–but I am talking about Christ and the church. However, each one of you also must love his wife as he loves himself, and the wife must respect her husband.*
—*Ephesians 5:31-33 (NIV)*

Be kind and compassionate to one another, forgiving each other, just as in Christ God forgave you.
—*Ephesians 4:32 (NIV)*

The Stuckeys and the Baileys. They epitomize our neighbors and co-workers. Couples just like them surround us every day, even sit beside us in church. Would you choose either of these couples as friends? Are these fictional characters the exception or the rule? Throughout the last few chapters, we have been invited into the inner sanctum of their family lives: close up and personal. The picture has been humorous in some instances, but overall not alluring.

As you recall, the Stuckeys have emotionally left each other behind in their relationship, and have bought into the lie that *"this is as good as it will ever get."* They are so "stuck" they resort regularly to manipulation and a series of rewards and punishment mechanisms in order to secure the meeting of their needs. Their marriage appears satisfactory on the surface, but on closer examination, the core is actually unstable. The question that might occur to us is, "What are they going to do when their teenage girls are gone from the home?" Statistics now show that a growing segment of the divorce population is among those married 25 years or more.[1] When the nest empties, many couples suddenly realize they no longer have a meaningful relationship. The distance between them is often so wide that finding a means to reconnect seems unattainable.

The Baileys have no such outward appearance; a careful assessment would show that they have serious flaws in their relationship. They are so dissimilar they see no road to reconciliation. They also have bought a lie: *they will never overcome their differences*, so it is not worth the effort. The only rational solution is to bail out.

They resort to isolation as a coping mechanism. Tiger works longer, stays away from home with his buddies, while Kitty lives in a world of fantasy—dreaming about the ideal home life she has envisioned since her childhood. She is clueless that Tiger is slowly seeking to work his way out of the relationship. Like so many struggling young brides, she thinks, "he will come around once we have children." She also may have thought, "I knew we were different." But DID SHE? Did *we?*

Both of these marriages are still unraveling: a satisfactory outcome for either of them appears to be nowhere in sight. The Baileys and the Stuckeys are not thriving; they are simply surviving! Through ignorance, they are allowing life within their relationships to ebb toward distance and despair.

The Mystery of Marriage

These stories, though fictional, are representative of the "state of the union" when it comes to the major issues surrounding marriage and money. As we have pointed out, the two key areas of marriage that lead to divorce, according to professional counselors, are: lack of communication and differences of opinion on the subject of finances.[2]

We submit an overarching reason: lack of understanding the "mystery of marriage," or the "mystery of differences." That mystery revolves around the fact that God has created us not only male and female, but that within every marriage significant differences exist, and that we must understand, accept and work toward magnifying—not minimizing—the strengths of each other. In preceding chapters we covered four inescapable areas of differences, using the Baileys and Stuckeys to "flesh out" scenes from ordinary life. Those areas were:

- 🕮 Problem solving together
- 🕮 Processing information together
- 🕮 Managing change together, and
- 🕮 Facing risk together

Now, the pressing question is: Why would God do this? Why would he intentionally design opposites to attract, knowing they would chafe and struggle, concluding differences to be a burden and not a blessing? Differences run the gamut from radical to moderate, but they yield similar challenges. Consider again the opening verses of this chapter:

> For this reason a man will leave his father and mother and be united to his wife, and the two will become one flesh. **_This is a profound mystery_**–but I am talking about Christ and the church. However, each one of you also must love his wife as he loves himself, and the wife must respect her husband.
> —Ephesians 5:31-33 (NIV)

The Apostle Paul here is directing our attention to a "profound mystery" — a radical riddle he applies to the relationship between

Jesus Christ and his bride, the Church. Immediately, he turns to the relationship between a man and woman within a marriage and employs the same description: it is a mystery. A husband is to love his wife as himself; a wife is to respect her husband. Both are onerous tasks, only possible by understanding God's design for differences, and his desire to empower and equip us to live out his divine design to our mutual benefit and his ultimate glory.

Stu, Dina, Tiger and Kitty lack understanding. They have missed God's plan for their differences. We have tried to depict them as composites of marriages we have encountered in our hundreds of hours of teaching and training on the subject of Love and Money. The Baileys and Stuckeys really are no different than the vast majority of marriages: polarized and out-of-balance. They don't even know what they don't know! Our question throughout this book has been, *"If what you thought to be true turned out not to be true, when would you want to know?"* Hopefully, that is why you accepted our offer to "listen in."

What these couples believed to be true is pretty much what all of us thought to be true when we got married: "This is going to be fun! All the sex we want, lots of time to spend with each other, great job, big house, nice kids—the good life." Well, that's a bit exaggerated, but most couples bring a host of unrealistic expectations—excess baggage is the usual term. A lack of teaching, counseling, no real relationship with God, and a host of other factors lead quickly to the stark realization that marriage is just plain hard work!

But any good thing worth having takes effort, time, resources, and perseverance. The glue that holds good marriages together is *commitment.* Remember the vow: "…for better, for worse, for richer, for poorer, in sickness or in health, to love and to cherish 'till death do us part?" Marriages lacking this foundation dissolve through a choice on the part of either of the spouses to simply end it or buckle down and just accept mediocrity—based on the belief that their differences are "irreconcilable." And, unfortunately, the laws of the land support this and make the dissolution of marriage as easy as changing a hairstyle. Some couples, rather than resort to divorce, live their lives as "married singles," their marriage a mere façade to the watching world. Their schedules, finances, friends and jobs are separate and often not even coordinated.

But are differences REALLY irreconcilable?

What if there really is a better way? What would you need to know in order to experience fresh wind, revitalization and reconciliation in your marriage?

The Law of Differences

Life is about choices. In one way, our lives are simply the product of all the choices we have made over time. Choices involve consequence. Viewed another way, choices consist of laws, laws that are irrevocable and irreversible. For example: the law of gravity. You may choose to hold an object in your hand or release it. If you allow the item to fall, it will hit the ground, simply because it is obeying the inescapable and irreversible law of gravity.

But if you chose to hold the object indefinitely, could you? No. Why? Because a secondary law is at work—fatigue. This law would then ensure the natural action would occur. But it began with a choice.

Within marriages, an invisible law is at work, a law that most never knew existed. We call it the *Law of Differences*. It, too, is inescapable—always at work, tugging away at your relationship, and either enhancing or diminishing its vitality.

We have seen this law surface in our fictitious characters; we have illustrated their approach to problem solving and their inability to move toward one another in an understanding way. In everyday life, how similar we all are when we preclude God's will and God's ways to work within us "...to will and to do of his good pleasure" (Philippians 2:13 KJV).

Consider the following illustration as we begin to dissect The Law of Differences and how the inescapable truths impact your marriage.

The Law of Differences
Choice

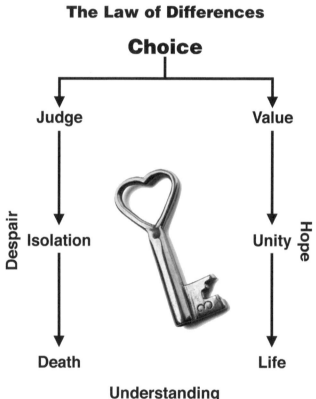

| Judge | Value |

Despair Isolation ... Unity **Hope**

Death ... Life

Understanding

Figure 1

Having followed the lives of our couples, analyzed their temperaments and reactions to various challenges, we propose that this was the basic force that was always at work under the surface of their marriages. Once understood, the application of these principles can transform homes and lives forever! Consider these words from the Old Testament:

> *This day I call heaven and earth as witnesses against you that*
> *I have set before you **life** and **death**, **blessings** and **curses**.*
> *Now **choose life**, so that you and your children may live.*
> *—Deuteronomy 30:19 (NIV)*

God, speaking through Moses, bids us consider life vs. death, and blessings vs. curses, ending with an admonishment for us to "choose life." Notice carefully that life, death, curse and blessing are the result of our volitional choices. It is highly interesting to understand, from the Hebrew text, the meaning of these words when translated into English. Blessing and curse carry the sense of "moving toward" or "stepping back" from something or someone.

- **Blessing** literally means "to ADD value or weight"
- **Curse** means "to SUBTRACT by damming up the stream"

Therefore we may conclude there are two avenues of choice set before us in our marriage relationship—in fact any relationship. In Figure 1, note that we choose to react to differences in one of two ways—resulting in dramatically different outcomes.

The Path To Death

Choosing this path begins with looking at one another through the *lens of weakness.* By that we mean that we focus or concentrate on one another's differences, especially those that create tension or frustrate us. We begin to **JUDGE** one another and posture ourselves to "be right." Disagreements over insignificant matters often lead to petty feuds and mental anguish. We may think, "My way is better." From the wise counsel of Moses, obviously this causes us to step back, not move toward one another.

Next, note in our illustration that judgment results in **ISOLATION.** Isolation may be either physical or emotional. Physical partitioning of living space only mirrors the emotional partitioning of the heart. Physical barriers may be erected as well as emotional barriers. Since the place we live out most of our marriage relationship is in the emotional realm, this sort of isolation is by far the more painful of the two. Couples living in judgment of one another and isolation from each another exhibit some of these characteristics:

- Spending more time with others than with each other (this often includes children—not always outsiders)
- Lack of meaningful communication
- Avoidance of one another ("am I invisible?")
- Filling time with trivial things to mask pain

This marriage model is lifeless, with daily routines marked by perfunctory, meaningless motions and harboring of secrets unsafe to share. Silence between spouses begins to stretch longer and longer. These couples live life in slow motion, and the termination of the union is inexorable—unless Divine intervention comes into play.

Ultimately, this path leads to **DEATH.** Loss of significance, romance and companionship produces **DESPAIR** as the most visible sign of a dying marriage. Infidelity and pornography often creep in, and divorce marks the final demise. Since we were created to connect, and we were created for companionship, it is understandable that humans would seek alternative sources of need fulfillment.

Proverbs 13:12 says that "Hope deferred makes the heart sick." Despair ought not to be! This is not God's created order. There is another path—another choice. Answers may be found within the spiritual life of each individual, carrying over into marriage and other relationships. We must learn to follow principles set forth by the Creator in his Word.

The Path To Life

Again, Moses said, *"choose life."* Why? His answer is "…that you and your children may live." This refers not to *physical* life and death, but *abundant* life. Jesus alludes to this in the New Testament when he explains that he came to give us "life more abundantly" (John 10:10). The quality of our lives, including the ability to feel joy and happiness, is deeply embedded in the truths of the Prophet's words. An "alive" marriage is easily distinguishable from a "lifeless" one, detectable in speech, attitudes, simple acts of kindness and etiquette, even on our countenances. The Scriptures say, "After all, no one ever hated his own body, but he feeds and cares for it, just as Christ does the church—for we are members of his body" (Ephesians 5:29,30).

How do we actively make this better choice? Let's turn our attention to the other side of our illustration.

It begins with **VALUING** one another, rather than judging. Here, we look at one another through the *lens of strength.* We allow our strengths, discovered through experience, interaction, assessments, or other means, to bring us to the place of mutual submission. This is God's plan for handling differences. Since it was his idea, we need to allow each other's strengths to blend together to produce something we can never produce individually. One of God's first pronouncements was, "It is not good for man to be alone" (Genesis 2:18). We previously expressed that truth in this formula: "one plus one equals one."

This is the true "Mystery of Marriage" —the "Mystery of Differences!"

Valuing and protecting one another within the calm core of commitment is God's ideal, and it leads to the place of **UNITY.** Here, the oneness that God purposed begins to become reality as we reflect God's glory within the bonds of our intimate relationship. The Psalmist said, "How good and pleasant it is when brothers *(including husbands and wives)* live together in unity" (Psalm 133:1). Once this occurs in marriage, there is no turning back: we cast off the old ways and do everything we can to maintain this harmony of hearts. Servitude and self-sacrifice become hallmarks of our partnership. This path of protection and acceptance leads ultimately to the final destination: life.

LIFE, as we have mentioned, is a choice. In Mark 5:24-35, the story of the woman who was healed from the issue of blood is recounted. She made a choice to press into the throng and touch the hem of Jesus' garment. The text says, "...and Jesus, immediately knowing in himself that *virtue had gone out of him*..." Healing virtue is life—God's life. Healing can be physical or emotional, and that healing can occur through common grace or "amazing grace."

Common grace involves the principles we have outlined in this section of the book. These are "tried and true" approaches to healing broken marriages. In Figure 1, the choice leading to life is filled with **HOPE,** not despair. Proverbs 13:12 goes on to say "...but a longing fulfilled is a tree of life." Do you long for a great marriage—one that truly is filled with hope and Christ's love? Hope is referred to in the Bible as "the anchor of the soul" (Hebrews 6:19). **Supernatural grace** is the touch of God, which brings life and wholeness to hearts and homes. Even in the midst of chaos, we can be hopeful, knowing that God is bigger than our problems, and that he is "up to something." God is present in the midst of conflict, even though we may be unaware of him. Often he has *purpose* for our pain.

The Key That Unlocks the Secret of The Law of Differences

Notice in Figure 1 there is a key. We have labeled this key **UNDERSTANDING.** Solomon, the wisest man who ever lived, made this pronouncement in Proverbs:

> *Blessed is the man who finds wisdom, the man who gains* **understanding,** *for she is more profitable than silver and yields better returns than gold. She is more precious than rubies; nothing you desire can compare with her. Long* **life** *is in her right hand; in her left hand are riches and honor. Her ways are pleasant ways, and all her paths are peace. She is a* **tree of life** *to those who embrace her; those who lay hold of her will be blessed.*
> —Proverbs 3:13-18

This is the promise of gaining understanding. Understanding leads to life. This unlocks the Law of Differences and moves us from independence on the left side of the illustration to interdependence on the right. Independence is the path away from God, and away from one another. Interdependence is the path toward God and toward one another, and actually cannot be achieved without DEPENDENCE upon God. Too many live in ignorance, unaware the Law of Differences is at work at all times in all situations.

To underscore our previous principle: differences are intended to complete us, not defeat us—help us, not hinder us!

But how does one change from the lens of judgment and weakness to the lens of valuing and strength? How do we gain the understanding necessary to move from the left side of the illustration to the right?

Through a simple act of **HUMILITY** we must approach one other and confess our ignorance and what it has produced in our marriage: judgment, isolation and despair. Then ask forgiveness for independent attitudes and actions, and make a commitment to live differently: to value, protect, and seek to understand one another in order to live as one, not two. Choose hope, life and interdependence. Choose to help one another through your individual strengths and differences. Pray together and become dependent upon God to pour out his virtue and life upon you: ask him for a "miracle marriage."

Remember this: if you push differences away, you lose something of great value!

What you choose to do with your differences from this day forward will either unite you or divide you.

You have a choice – chose life!

As we transition to Part II, we remind you that one of the major causes of stress among spouses is conflict over money. We want to strengthen marriages not only from an emotional and relational standpoint, but also from a practical standpoint, by teaching truth regarding how to manage resources entrusted to us by God.

We will include topics such as the dangers of wealth, issues revolving around consumer credit, financing of automobiles, retirement, and mortgages.

Money, money, money. Are you ready?

The Marriage Insights Profile

We would like to close this chapter and Part I of the book by giving our readers an opportunity to move the concepts outlined in this part of the book from theory to application. While we have spoken broadly here about differences, in less than 10 minutes you can become far more specific. The *Marriage Insights Profile* is a 24-page report on your individual and relational strengths that is generated from an online assessment that is completed in only 8-10 minutes; your personal results will then be provided immediately.

The Profile is packed full of valuable insights and information that will help identify your strengths and those of your spouse, and clearly identify your differences. On the basis of your individual Profile data, and the teaching in Part 1 of this book, a dialogue can be initiated to help move you toward blending your differences to produce what God intended: unity and oneness in your marriage.

For pricing information, and to complete the *Marriage Insights Profile,* go to www.loveandmoney.org and click the link that says, "I am reading the book."

Marriage Insights Profile Overview

As we have suggested, sharing reports with each other will clarify how you complement your spouse's God-given strengths. This, in turn, can create an opportunity to affirm your mate's special qualities, and provide communication insights to increase oneness and decrease conflict.

The *Marriage Insights Profile* includes the following sections:

- ৯ Start Here! – brief overview of the report contents.
- ৯ Introduction – explanation of the meanings of the letters in your Style Analysis Graph and brief description of the basic character traits.
- ৯ Your Style Analysis Graph – graphical depiction of your "core" style in four predictable areas: problem solving, processing information, managing change, and facing risk.
- ৯ General Characteristics – general statements to provide a broad understanding of the strengths and behavioral style you bring to your marriage.
- ৯ Keys to Motivating – statements of your wants or values that can provide understanding of what motivates you.
- ৯ Relationship Strengths – identifies specific talents and strengths that you bring to your marriage and relationships.
- ৯ Keys to Communication – describes how you like your spouse and others to communicate with you.
- ৯ Barriers to Communication – describes what NOT to do when relating to you.
- ৯ Communicating with Others – provides suggestions on methods to improve your communications with others.

ೞ Hindering Factors – list of possible hindering factors with regard to your marriage relationship.

ೞ One-Word Descriptors – words that may describe you in the four predictable areas.

ೞ Perceptions – provides additional information on your self-perception and how others may perceive your actions.

ೞ Action Plan – guide for preparing a plan to improve communication.

ೞ Additional Insights – introduction and explanation of how much you feel you may need to "adapt" your "core" style to match the needs or requirements of your home environment and to fit your unique marriage relationship.

ೞ Style Analysis Graphs – graphical depiction on your "core" style and your "adapted" style in the four predictable areas.

ೞ How Are You Having to "Adapt"? – a list of descriptions of how you may feel you need to respond to the current environment to be accepted.

ೞ Core and Adapted Style – information related to the stress and pressure you may feel when you "adapt" your style to your home environment.

ೞ The Ministry Insights Wheel – explanation and graphical depiction to analyze and compare with your spouse.

Part 2
Money The Great Divide

Chapter **8**

The Dangers of Riches

*...give me neither poverty nor riches! Give me just enough to
satisfy my needs. For if I grow rich, I may deny you and say,
'Who is the Lord?' And if I am too poor, I may steal and thus
insult God's holy name.*
—*Proverbs 30:8,9 (NLT)*

The story is told of a businessman traveling abroad who was at
the pier of a small coastal village when a small boat with just one
fisherman docked. Inside the small boat were several large yellow fin
tuna. The businessman complimented the local native on the quality
of his fish and asked how long it took to catch them. The fisherman
replied, "Only a little while." The man then asked, "Why didn't you stay
out longer and catch more fish?" The sun-baked fisherman told him
he had more than enough to support his family's needs for the day.

The businessman continued, "But what do you do with the rest of
your time?" The fisherman said, "I sleep late, play with my children,
take a siesta every afternoon with my wife, stroll into the village each
evening, where I sip wine and play guitar with my amigos. I have a
full, busy, satisfied life, señor."

The business executive furrowed his brow and scoffed, "I have
a Harvard MBA and I could help you become rich! You should spend
more time fishing and with the proceeds, buy a bigger boat. With

the proceeds from the bigger boat you could buy *several* boats, and eventually you would have a *fleet* of fishing boats. Instead of selling your catch to a middleman you could sell directly to the processor and eventually open your own cannery. You would then control the product, processing and distribution. You would have it all. Of course, you would have to leave this small fishing village and move to Mexico City, then L.A. and eventually New York City, where you would run your expanding enterprise."

The fisherman asked, "But señor, how long will this take?"

To which the executive replied, "15-20 years if you're lucky."

"But what then, señor?"

The businessman laughed and said, "That's the best part. When the time is right you would announce an IPO and sell your company stock to the public and become very rich. You would make *millions*."

"Millions, señor? Then what?"

He said, "Then you could retire. Move to a small coastal fishing village where you would sleep late, fish a little, play with your grand kids, take siestas with your wife, stroll through the village in the evenings, where you could sip wine and play your guitar with your amigos."[1]

We have lost our moorings. Do you find yourself *wanting* to identify with the island fisherman, but *knowing* you are more like the Harvard MBA, even though you may lack his credentials? This modern day parable reveals this stark truth: most of us believe that *cold cash warms the heart!* When money comes into our possession—when it falls into our hands—our fingers begin to curl, and a "chemical process" sets in. A pleasant sensation begins to course through our veins and into our torso—finally winding itself around our hearts, until the enemy of our souls exclaims, "Gotcha!"

Introduction to Part 2

Part 1, the Love and Marriage portion of *Love and Money,* began with the dangers associated with differences in marriage, and how to begin to properly and biblically view those differences. In Part 2 we turn our attention to money matters—beginning first with the dangers surrounding wealth. From the parable above, it is clear that we need a paradigm shift—a new perspective on wealth and the dangers they pose when passionately pursued. "The love of money is the root of all kinds of evil," assert the Scriptures (1 Timothy 6:10). This constitutes a warning to us—a danger sign—and we would be wise to pay heed to it. We will examine several concepts that will help us understand those dangers, and then devise a plan of action throughout the remainder of Part 2 to help correct our course where we may have strayed from the Biblical path. The Stuckeys and Baileys only mirror for us the possible state of our own lives and our need to pursue the path of obedience to God's mandates; therefore, we will examine practical procedures to help shape not only our thinking, but our abilities to manage the resources entrusted to us by God.

Since the depression of the 1920's, the United States has been on an upward spiral of debt and wealth accumulation that has never been equaled in history. Wealth and debt are so common that a whole new set of expectations and social issues have been created, addressing matters with which we as a society have never dealt. On any given evening on television, numerous commercials advertise services promising to eliminate a consumer's burden of debt. Even if success is achieved, the chances of repeating the cycle are immense.

This matrix of riches—wealth and debt—has great seductive powers and is the siren call of the world, pulling us in its direction. Note that God has prohibited us from aspiring to the acquisition of wealth (1 Timothy 6:9). Debt is an important part of this equation because it *fuels artificial wealth and gives the illusion of riches.* Due to the influences of our past, our experiences, our understanding and our culture, we are ill equipped to combat this challenge. It is obvious that we need to "renew our minds" (Romans 12:2) through an understanding of God's perspective—learning to see things as he sees them.

In this chapter we want to investigate the Biblical teaching surrounding the dangers associated with money and how they can affect our marriages, our jobs, the way we raise our children—the very way we live our lives. The Baileys and the Stuckeys have clearly run over some speed bumps in their marriages that have been caused by disagreements, misunderstandings or differences in their approach to the handling of their family accounts. Before we transition in the next section to practical matters of managing resources, we need to more broadly define the problem.

Tiger Bailey is busy "deal-making," hoping for the "big one" he thinks will solve everything (we call this the" lottery mentality"). He's "going for the gold," seemingly excluding God from the equation as he navigates his way through the deepening demands of life. As an aspiring young leader, he has embraced this destructive deception: "It's all about ME!" Someone has rightly labeled this generation as the "entitlement generation."

Sporting a freshly laundered consumer mentality, Dina Stuckey is often off to the mall to "shop 'til she drops." For a few hours per month she escapes the pressures of her job, family and other responsibilities, as the lure of another world beckons her. The fragrances of the cosmetics department, the beauty of the clothing department and the glitter of the jewelry—though tempting—provide an exhilarating sensory catharsis for her. Many times, she adds a few things she "deserves" to her shopping cart ("I got them on sale" is her motto!). But…isn't Dina just like US? And isn't Tiger simply a reflection of many of US? If we are completely transparent, we must admit that these same forces are at work in us. We, too, long for some relief from the massive pressures that mount up during the week (that jingle keeps ringing in our ears, "you deserve a break today").

Dina knows Stu will stew and a storm will brew when she comes home to the familiar "discussion" that inevitably follows one of her "deserved" shopping sprees. Stu is focused more on the future, while she lives more in the present. And Tiger, like Dina, wants all the "stuff," and is willing to work long and hard to make sure he gets it! ("I'm just trying to provide for my family!") For both of them, the answer to the question, "How much is enough?" is, "Just a little bit more." Tiger and Kitty also have their "moments of dissonance"—slowly coming to realize they not only have differences in personality and temperament, but great dissimilarities in their outlook and approach to money. They have to maintain separate checking accounts, because Kitty is so unorganized that she is unable to keep hers balanced. Tiger refuses to be associated with such lack of responsibility, and often reminds her of it. First, marriage issues, and now money issues…

And that is **precisely** why we must carefully examine the dangers of riches "under the microscope." You may be amazed at what we find.

Four Deadly "C" Words

The American economic system—the arena in which our couples must live and conduct their lives—is based on four concepts that build on one another:

1. Comparison
2. Contentment (or lack thereof)
3. Covetousness
4. Competition

These principles each have a positive side, but their negative aspects seem to shape our thinking, and especially the business environment in which we spend over one-third of our lives. First, we are encouraged, largely through the media, to **compare** ourselves with one another (you know we have to keep up with the Jones). We do this when we enter someone's home, we engage in it when we go to someone else's office, ride in another car, or take care of someone else's children (can you believe we even compare our children?). In this foolish exercise, we either compare favorably, which leads to pride, or unfavorably, which leads to self-pity. *Comparison is the favorite indoor sport of America,* but there are no real winners in this game. Play it at your own risk!

Comparison usually leads to a **lack of contentment.** Actually, retailers are *counting* on comparison when you walk through the mall—last year's model certainly needs to be replaced with *this* year's model! This is called "planned obsolescence." Things are designed and planned to break down, fade, and go out of style. Without comparing our old one with the new one, we would not come to the conclusion that what we have is no longer of value. The writer of Hebrews admonishes us:

> Keep your lives free from the love of money and be content with what you have, because God has said, Never will I leave you; never will I forsake you."
> —Hebrews 13:5 (NIV)

The failure to be content may be the chief cause of our society's mind-boggling consumer debt, as well as the driving force behind our accumulation mentality. Lack of contentment leads further to **covetousness**—we want what our neighbor has—their goods, their lifestyle, even their health! We may even covet what our competitor in business has—his market share, or the new product he has just developed. His sales are up, yours are down. Our appetites are insatiable. If the truth were told, wouldn't we all want "just a little bit more?"

And that leads us to the final "c word" — **competition.** While there are healthy types of competition, the type that seeks to conquer at everyone else's expense is unhealthy and destructive. In a later chapter we will investigate the truth about work, and see that it is an arena in which to minister to people, not manipulate them to our own ends. There is something terribly wrong with the picture of a father shouting at his son to "smash his face in the dirt" while trying to teach him fairness in the pursuit of athletic sportsmanship. When we view others only through the lens of what we can extract from them—how they can help us—we denigrate them, robbing them of the glory that God bestowed upon them at their creation. We must constantly question our motives, crying out with the Psalmist, "Search me, O God, and know my heart" (Psalm 139:23).

Is your life full of compassion and contentment or covetousness and competition? It is at these crossroads that you will find the answers to many of life's questions in your marriage and your money.

A Question of Motives

Boyd Bailey (no relationship to Tiger or Kitty), in his daily email devotional "Right Thinking," has this to say about one type of motivator—money:

> *Money motivation is not the best motivation. In fact it can make you downright miserable. It makes you miserable and those who surround you. Money motivated people are never content. They have an insatiable desire for the next deal, or the next opportunity to make more. An overriding desire for money leads you to compromise common sense*

*and character. Ironically, your family suffers the
most even when you want them to enjoy the benefits
money may produce. Moreover, money motivated
individuals stoop as low as using the Lord to line
their pockets. Religion and church become a means
for more money. This angers God. He is moved by
righteous indignation when His bride is prostituted
for worldly purposes. The church is a conduit for
Christ not a clearinghouse for economic gain. He is
greatly grieved when money becomes the driving
force of any institution or individual.[2]*

We cannot escape the fact that there are proper and improper uses of money, and the improper use poses problems for us. Knowing intuitively that we have never actually had a pure motive, what are the sources of our erroneous value system? If we accept the message of the media and other cultural communications, wealth is presented as a panacea for the totality of our woes. Once again, we draw your attention to the premise that *what we believe to be true may not be true!* So, what is the truth about money? What are the specific dangers? We will analyze first the overriding *principle* governing all possessions, and then the *purpose* of possessions.

The Paramount Principle Governing All Possessions

In chapter 1, we set forth four foundational presuppositions upon which *Love and Money* is based, the most important of which is: ***All that you have belongs to God and comes from God.*** God is the owner of all wealth, and he dispenses it as he chooses. He gives it and he takes it away as he pleases. If we were to poll an audience as to where their provision came from, nearly everyone would respond, "From God." But there seems to be a gulf between what we believe and how we live. If we believe God is the Owner and the Provider, then why do we live as though we have what we have because we *earned* it or because we *deserve* it, neither of which is true? The Apostle Paul poses this thought-provoking question:

> ... What do you have that God hasn't given you? And if everything you have is from God, why boast as though it were not a gift?
> —1 Corinthians 4:7 (NLT)

James, in his epistle, graciously provides us with an answer:

> Every good and perfect gift is from above, coming down from the Father of the heavenly lights...
> —James 1:17 (NIV)

The obvious conclusion is: all that we have came from the hand of God as a gift of his grace. Therefore, it is not what we *have* but how we *respond* to what we have that counts most to God. It is neither man's purpose nor responsibility to alter God's plan of distribution by "hard work and shrewd thinking," but to steward what God gives. If God is the owner, then we are his agents or "asset managers"—we have a portion of his total portfolio entrusted to our care. Some day we will stand before God to give an account as to how we handled his funds! There are an abundance of parables in the Bible that illustrate this reality. *Faithfulness to opportunity* and not *production* is what pleases God, and it is upon that basis that Jesus Christ at the "Judgment Seat of Christ" will judge us (1 Corinthians 3:11-15).

Remember: riches are a *temporal* commodity, while our handling of resources is of *eternal* consequence. It is not how we do in comparison to someone else, but what we do with our own gifts, time, energy, health, abilities, aptitudes, background, influence—as well as material goods—that will make a difference in eternity. God will compensate for individual differences at that moment, since he is the one who originally distributed the gifts to each of us for His glory.

The Purpose of Possessions

As we focus on the material goods—the portfolio—entrusted to us as God's asset managers, note that the Scriptures give a threefold purpose for these possessions.

Basic Needs: our required food, clothing and shelter. As we have said, God reserves the right to determine and define the dimensions of our basic needs (Matthew 6:23-33).

Celebration of Life: Our relationship with God as we enjoy what he has provided, including beauty, art, creation and recreation (1 Timothy 6:17-19; 2 Corinthians 9:6-8).

Service: The focus of our riches in the direction of ministry and the meeting of the needs of others around us (Matthew 28:18-20; Mark 10:43-45: Philippians 2:3,4; 2 Corinthians 9:13-15).

The Stuckeys and the Baileys have no frame of reference for an understanding of this. If you were to ask them the question, "Why do you go to work?" their answer would probably be, "to earn a living." Beyond meeting basic needs, they do not have a category for celebration or service. And we have not yet mentioned anything about charitable giving. The Stuckeys consider themselves respectable church members, but Stu is not very active. Dina is the one who is at church every time the door is open. Stu dislikes messages on giving, and feels that Dina gives so much of her time that giving money is up to those who are doing nothing. The Baileys go to church when convenient, but view church as one of the "fashionable" organizations they belong to in order to be seen. They think it's great that there are no dues! "You can't give what you do not have," says Tiger.

It is important to bear in mind that these Biblical passages focus on two things: *people* and *eternity*. How many giving and spending decisions do YOU make with solid Biblical principles in mind? Based on a review of these and other pertinent passages, the following truths become evident:

- The three Biblical uses of possessions mentioned earlier are the **only** reasons for which God gives us material resources. There are no others. We may have other uses for money—gaining a sense of worth, influence, paying the utility bill, saving for retirement—but God only endorses these three.

- *Basic needs are determined between God and each individual.* Each of us will be held accountable to God for the basis upon which we make that determination. None of us has the right to judge another in matters of lifestyle, habits or other non-essentials. Whatever convictions we hold must not to be considered normative for other people.

- *Anything we receive beyond basic needs is not to become the level of our expectation from God.* The level of our lifestyle today cannot become our expectation for tomorrow. God may drastically reduce our status or income and still be meeting our basic needs according to his divine design. It is interesting to note that we do not question God when he gives us more than we need. A problem arises when we begin to view abundance only as his blessing instead of his means to bless others.

- *Anything God provides a follower of Christ above basic needs carries with it increased levels of responsibility and accountability.* Make no mistake—increased levels of material resources can work to our disadvantage as well as to our advantage. Scripture is clear. "From everyone who has been given much, much will be demanded; and from the one who has been entrusted with much, much more will be asked." (Luke 12:48 NIV)

Riches certainly may be viewed as a blessing—along with all good gifts from God—but with them come obligations and Biblical expectations. The more we have, the more accountable we become for what he has given us.

    ❧ *Anytime we experience a shift in God's provision from one standard to another, it may cause stress in our lives.* Our response to the level of God's provision is quite important to the Creator. Our capacity to persist will largely be determined by our view of God's commitment to our well being and His promise to provide for us. Debt sometimes occurs when we refuse to accept the shift, and override it by once again resorting to the meeting of our own needs.

    ❧ *In the celebration of life category, the line between enjoyment and indulgence is blurry, and must be determined individually and prayerfully before God.* Since we all have difficulty determining this in our own lives, we cannot possibly hope to do so in the lives of others. Although this is not our purview, we nevertheless indulge in this practice. There is a natural (and Biblical) tension in trying to determine where to draw this line. It seems to be designed by God to produce a level of dependence upon him to set the course of our standard of living.

    ❧ *We are to give as a part of our service to God, not simply because he commanded it, but because we are grateful.* This demonstrates to him that our value system is in alignment with his. Our giving has nothing to do with solving problems in God's kingdom; he is quite capable of taking care of his own business. We are not doing God a "favor" by giving to the building of his kingdom. On the contrary, he is doing US a favor by allowing us the privilege of participating in his work through giving. God's children should re-visit the issue of charitable giving, and grasp the principle we have underscored here: he owns it all. If God is the owner, we aren't "giving" anything that is not already his! The question is not, "How much should I give?" but rather, "How much should I keep?" The answer to the first question is, "Give it all, since he is the owner." The answer to the second is, "Ask God how he wants you to manage his accounts." The Bible says God loves a "cheerful giver" (2 Corinthians 9:7).

The Pursuit of Wealth

Scripture continually warns God's people concerning the dangers of desiring and pursuing wealth. Paul minces no words when he penned this to Timothy:

> People who want (desire) to get rich fall into temptation and a trap and into many foolish and harmful desires that plunge men into ruin and destruction. For the love of money is a root of all kinds of evil. Some people, eager for money, have wandered from the faith and pierced themselves with many griefs.
> —1 Timothy 6:9,10 (NIV)

In Luke's Gospel, we are admonished to "beware of greed," remembering that our lives do not consist in the "abundance of our possessions" (Luke 12:15). In the Timothy passage above, the weight of the warning is emphasized through the use of "couplets"— the doubling of phrases for affect: "temptation AND a trap"; "foolish AND harmful desires"; "ruin AND destruction." Since this warning is addressed to the "rich," we need to definitely delineate the audience.

Who, exactly, IS rich? We tend to assign the term to those who have more than we do.

The Stuckeys, for example, do not consider themselves rich nor greedy, but it depends on whom they *compare* themselves to. Could the incident involving the red convertible illustrate any of the dangerous "C" words? Whatever the size of their bank accounts, or whatever their standard of living, when compared to those who have more than they do, they conclude they are not rich.

The Baileys *know* they aren't rich but live as they were. Their consumer debt leaves no doubt in their minds they aren't rich, but they carefully conceal this from others. Tiger feels he has a foolproof formula to become rich before he turns 40, and until he arrives there he painstakingly projects the appearance of wealth. He needs to see and seize the Timothy truth: he could be "plunged into ruin and destruction" as a result of his inordinate drive to become wealthy!

We can hear someone saying, "But I don't want to be rich, I just want to be 'comfortable'!" Is there really any difference? It still begs the question, "How much is enough?" People who "want to get rich" (NIV) are, "those who have an excessive desire to acquire wealth…" A simpler word for that is GREED. Again, it pointedly says *we are not to desire riches.* The word "desire" in this context means "to make it our purpose or to will it." It is more than "wishing"—it is the focus of our will.

An appetite for the accumulation of wealth can become the driving force of our hearts, consequently elevating the gift above the giver. In Tiger Baileys case, he always focused on those things in his life over which he felt he had control. He tried to control Kitty, but gave up on his scheme, realizing it wasn't going to happen. She was once his primary focus: he pursued her and married her, thinking he would be able to mold her over time. But then he moved his focus to the acquisition of riches, which he considered more achievable, counting his relational loss to be of lesser value.

"Riches," as we are applying the term here, means, "provision above our basic needs." Pursuing wealth means we make it our prime occupation or objective, obscuring the real reasons for which God gives us material resources. The harder we work for it, the less we seem to enjoy it. We began this chapter with this Proverb:

> ..give me neither poverty nor riches! Give me just enough to satisfy my needs. For if I grow rich, I may deny you and say, 'Who is the Lord?' And if I am too poor, I may steal and thus insult God's holy name.
>
> —Proverbs 30:8,9 (NLT)

This is the only proper prayer found in the Bible concerning wealth or riches. Jesus said, "Give us today our daily bread." Paul said God wants to meet your NEEDS. Solomon says to pray for only enough to sustain you: neither poverty NOR riches. If you doubt the validity of this verse, think about this: if you have money in the bank, do you think about God more, or less? If there is "too much month left at the end of the money," do you pray more or pray less? When you pray about your money situation do you pray for more money or less?

With this foundation for understanding the hazards riches can create, let's summarize our discussion of this point into five specific dangers, all of which are the result of the subtle deceptions and lies which have become part of our modern mind set.

Five Dangers Defined

1. **Riches can create a false sense of independence and security.** Independence is the path leading away from God, and we are never less secure than when we think we are independent from Him and have no need for Him. Jesus said it is hard for a rich man to get into heaven (Matthew 19:23). Why? Because with the abundance of wealth comes the perception of control. To the degree we feel we are in control of the issues and circumstances surrounding our lives we develop an attitude of independence, which is simply an *illusion.*

2. **Riches can deceive a person into thinking that his finances have been brought under the Lordship of Christ.** It is easy for Christians to simply superimpose Christianity over their existing value systems. When the paycheck is steady, we may exhibit a spirit of generosity and freely give to God's work. Our security easily becomes based on financial prosperity. But suppose we read verses like Matthew 19:21-22 ("...sell your possessions and give to the poor..."). Would we balk at that possibility if God were to ask us to do that? If we are unwilling to consider this, we should question the level of our commitment to Christ. If our income decreases, and our relationship with God falters at the same time, our possessions have become our standard of expectation of God's blessing and provision, and have not been given over to the Lordship of Christ.

3. **Riches can create a non-Biblical sense of self worth and significance.** As we have mentioned, Jeremiah the prophet reminds us that our worth is to come from God's *declaration* of our worth (Jeremiah 9:23,24),

not because of what we have, what we do or what we achieve. We sometimes view life as a blank slate building equity. When young, we felt significant when we had $5.00 ($1.00?) in our pocket and gas in the car! Money creates fuzzy thinking about our importance—it may take more than $5.00 now, but the tendency and danger is still there. Even though we are depraved, God says we are of so much value to him that he bought us with a great price—his own Son—Jesus Christ.

4. **Riches can tempt us with the sin of greed and covetousness.** Riches prime the pump of greed—that aspect of our old nature that simply craves more and more.

Consider these truths about desiring money:

- Whoever loves money will not be satisfied with more
- The desire for money is insatiable, like all appetites
- The desire for money may make us selfish, and cause us to use and exploit people for personal gain
- The desire for more money produces worry and anxiety

In Philippians 4:6-7, the word anxiety means, "a need that distracts," or "double-mindedness." When energy is divided between trying to "get your share" and "keep what you have," the motto becomes: "The one who dies with the most toys wins." Actually the one who dies with the most still dies! If we live long enough to accumulate many things we will learn that the more we have the more time it will take to maintain them. Possessions drain us of not only time, but of emotional, physical, and spiritual energy.

Statistics reveal the poor are more generous than the rich (measured as a percentage of their wealth). You would think that those who find themselves rich in this world—who have their basic needs met—could therefore afford to be more generous than the rest of us. To explain this, understand the phenomenon that the appetite for wealth is immeasurable. In Matthew's Gospel, we read these words:

> *Do not store up for yourselves treasures on earth, Where moth and rust destroy, and where thieves break in and steal. But store up for yourselves treasures in heaven, Where moth and rust do not destroy, and where thieves do not break in and steal. For where your treasure is, there your heart will be also.*
> *—Matthew 6:19-21 (NIV)*

It seems there is a direct connection between our wallets and our hearts. We trust our deposits in the bank of earth more than we trust deposits in the bank of heaven, principally because we don't understand the currency of heaven.

We said earlier that *people* and *God's Word* last forever; therefore, deposits in our eBank account (eternal) are measured in souls, not dollars. Violation of these Matthew commandments occurs when we transfer trust from the *provider* to the *provision* itself. "Storing up" connotes "hoarding"—the fear that in a time of need God will not be able to "come through for us." In our chapter on work we will emphasize that we are to concentrate our efforts on making deposits in our heavenly bank accounts by "making disciples," not "making money."

5. **Riches can be viewed as a means to simplify a person's life.** The older we become, the greater the desire to create a hassle-free, simple lifestyle. In succeeding chapters, we will deal with issues of wealth management, retirement accounts, and other financial instruments. But we must first question the legitimacy of viewing retirement mentally, physically and spiritually, as a valid Biblical goal or purpose, since retirement is not explicitly stated in Scripture.

Although a simple life may have legitimate expressions, the danger of this concept is that it may be an attempt to eliminate the need to walk by faith. *To eliminate walking by faith through simplification of lifestyle is another deception of riches.* We should never desire to control our own environment and future simply to eradicate uneasiness, since faith is *essential* to please God (Hebrews 11:6).

To eliminate entanglement (debt, for example) is legitimate; to eliminate faith is not. The key is right focus: simplification in order to serve God and others. To conclude our thinking about this principle, consider what we are NOT saying:

> ✤ *First, we are not suggesting that a person is to be foolish with his finances (since they really belong to God).* We are accountable as managers of the resources given to us by God. The manipulation of circumstances to accumulate riches today, in order to eliminate the uncertainty of tomorrow is both pointless and dangerous. Paul says not to place our hope in the "uncertainty of riches" (1 Timothy 6:17-19).

> ✤ *Second, we are not suggesting that a person should abstain from paying his debts!* We are saying that real wisdom and discernment are needed in this area. To eliminate debt simply to be in control, secure our future, gain a sense of peace, eradicate hassles or do away with faith leads to the dangerous desire for inordinate wealth as an end in itself. The proper motive for paying debt is to discharge our God-given responsibilities, not achieve financial independence.

> ✤ *Third, we are not saying that a person should be cavalier or irresponsible concerning his finances.* It is obvious that we should act responsibly toward

the issue of debt, investments, the payment of monthly bills, saving for children's education and so on. We will soon address these issues, but they *must be based on an understanding of these Biblical principles.*[3]

What if what you thought to be true turned out not to be true? Remember the story of the fisherman? He was being advised to build a larger fleet in order to accumulate more wealth. But the fisherman understood there was no purpose behind it. Wealth for the sake of wealth is wrong. He knew he already had more than he needed. Don't you? What should you do with what you already have? Are you being faithful? Do you really need a bigger fishing fleet?

Do you listen more to Wall Street than to God?

The Stuckeys and the Baileys need some practical help. Do you?

Chapter 9

Types of Money

Moreover it is required in stewards, that a man be found faithful.
—1 Corinthians 4:2 (KJV)

Don't hoard treasure down here where it gets eaten by moths and corroded by rust or—worse!—stolen by burglars. Stockpile treasure in heaven, where it's safe from moth and rust and burglars. It's obvious, isn't it? The place where your treasure is, is the place you will most want to be, and end up being.
—Matthew 6:19-21 (The Message)

"Where on earth did you get that idea?!" That pronouncement probably reverberated in both the Starkey and Bailey households like the dying echo of a bad musical chord, whenever financial pressures boiled to the surface. Polls-apart opinions separate spouses not only emotionally, but sometimes physically, as feuds finally give way to slamming doors, avoiding further attempts at resolution. Those same sorts of scenes may have crept into YOUR marriage as discussions of money differences facilitated the fading of the honeymoon glow.

When it comes to the subject of money, our views, opinions, and practices are forged from a number of sources. Early in our lives we are exposed to family and friends' views and methods of handling money, and, like so many other family practices, we emulate them.

Later in life, we may re-examine those practices and adopt other systems. And in doing so, we may develop an entirely new set of problematic practices.

Make no mistake: *money has a strange effect on people*. As we learned in Chapter 8, if you touch a person's wallet, you touch his heart! What one person considers normative relative to accruing and managing wealth may be vastly different for another.

We want to begin in these next chapters to outline some simple principles and practices that the Stuckeys and Baileys sorely needed to understand, and which might have helped them avoid conflict in the various scenarios presented. Our intent is that these fundamentals will also help YOU!

Also in Chapter 8, we illustrated the difference between a "Wall Street" mindset and a simpler "fisherman" attitude, contrasting the pursuit of wealth for the sake of wealth vs. pursuit of money for the sake of provision and wise planning. Let's examine our two couples more closely and try to discover whether they fit the "Captain of Industry" mold or the more practical fisherman model.

The Stuckey's Approach to Money

Stu Stuckey, if asked, would understand the financial term "opportunity cost," (which we will discuss momentarily) from a technical standpoint, which gives him a different perspective on how difficult it is to save and invest. As a corporate financial executive, he knows that one day in the future his family will rely on those savings. His wife, Dina, has no such grasp of this concept. She shops simply to fill an emotional void. She is very American, since shopping for the pleasure of shopping is a national pastime. As a culture, we have gone far beyond shopping out of necessity to that of acquiring for the sake of stockpiling. The first thing we need to understand about money is that everything has a **true cost** as well as an **opportunity**

cost, which is what the funds could have earned had they been handled more wisely.

It is obvious from our up close and personal time with the Stuckeys, to say that Stu is a **saver** and Dina a **spender**. This is true in most marriages—couples find themselves at opposite ends of the spectrum when it comes to spending/saving. Once again, we encounter the issue of differences. In Part 1 of this book, we sought to help readers understand their differences within their marriage; now, in Part 2, we want to apply those same insights to the financial dimension of marriage. In some cases, **both** spouses are spenders rather than savers, which can put a *tremendous strain* on each of them, since finances are such a "daily" part of life. The same might be true in the case of two savers! Conflict is inevitable; balance is the goal.

The Bailey's Approach to Money

The Baileys, on the other hand, are very educated, but their training and background excluded any instruction concerning money matters, especially the concept of lost opportunity cost. You will recall that Tiger wants to project an image in his sphere of influence—one of status and success. Therefore, he tries to "buy that image" through his spending habits: what he drives, what he wears, where he lives and what he possesses. He has no idea that the very image he is financing, via consumer credit, has a higher price tag than he realizes.

Understanding this financial principal could go a long way in helping the Baileys with the financial burdens they face: credit card debt, school loans, large apartment lease, and car payments. Tiger (like Dina Stuckey) might be less tempted to buy immediately if he really understood the consequence his current spending will have on his future. Likewise, Kitty needs to grasp the importance of getting out of debt before she pushes Tiger any further toward acquisition of a new home. Finally, in chapter 6, Tiger realized his need for a long-range solution to their debt and laid that plan before his bride, assuring her that the purchase of a home was indeed part of their future. An important shift in his thinking occurred: his NOW attitude gave way to a LATER attitude. (We can't help wondering, however, based on Tiger's past history, just how long his new strategy will last.)

Understanding the Concept of Opportunity Cost

Once the concept of opportunity cost is comprehended, it may be taken to an extreme. For example, there is an opportunity cost attached to the food we eat, but it would be inadvisable to stop spending money on food to save or invest those funds. Everything you buy has an opportunity cost, but here we want to focus your attention on the things you purchase that you can do something about. You cannot eliminate food costs, but you CAN adjust the frequency of eating out—spending twice as much as you would if you were to eat at home. The opportunity cost is the difference between the two.

Like most things in life, the issue is *balance*. If your lifestyle consists mainly of consuming much of your financial resources, and you seem unable save anything, you have an obstacle to overcome. Conversely, if you are so focused on your future and accruing wealth that you are unable to live a meaningful life today, you also face a dilemma. By avoiding losses (transferring money away unnecessarily), and becoming more efficient with your resources, you could solve problems in both your accumulated assets, as well as your immediate lifestyle funds.

At this point, it is important to understand how your unique design, and your spouse's uniqueness impacts how you each view the concept of capital AND your mutual financial portfolio. Potential conflicts in marriage arise from the fact that there are different types of money. These differences play out differently for each of us, depending on the level of understanding of financial principles and practices. Previously, we saw that our differences are designed by God to help, not hinder us; therefore, we conclude that we can blend our financial differences to formulate something agreeable, exciting and unique.

Part of the "excess baggage" spouses bring into a marriage include differing opinions of how money really works, which creates conflict. This major mishap of marriage can be overcome by gaining a better understanding of sound financial principles.

But first we must understand a fundamental principle: *all money is not the same.*

Two General Categories of Money

Most people are probably aware of these two general types of money:

- Money we <u>spend</u>, or **lifestyle money**, and
- Money we <u>save</u>, or **accumulated money**

In 2006 facts indicated that for the first time in history the average American was actually spending more than he made. The savings rate then was negative, but since the recent economic turndown savings have actually begun to rise. This is an alarming statistic in many ways, but it is even more frightening when considering the impact this has on the average person's ability to give to charitable causes. For a follower of Jesus Christ, **giving** is another type of money that we include as part of our lifestyle funds. For many believers "giving" (sometimes called "tithing") is that amount *left over* after our spending and savings. With savings rates at a historical low there is little wonder why giving is suffering.

While this chapter is not intended to instill guilt about anyone's current giving habits, there may be something God wants to do in us to improve our ability to responsibly handle monies entrusted to us. Holy Scripture says that giving is to come from a joyful heart.

It is our intention in the second half of this book to help readers understand *how money functions,* which can relieve stress and improve other areas of life. It makes little sense to educate someone regarding the principles of accumulation without including instruction on how or why there is a need to save and give. We will examine financial strategies that will help you develop a solid plan. Ask yourself these questions: Is your money doing all it can do? On a scale of 1-10 (ten being the highest) how would you rate **your** expertise in managing money? (If you answered less than 10, keep reading.)

Just as improving marital communication strengthens the *love* portion of marriage, we believe that meaningful dialogue also improves the *financial* dimension. Knowing your spouse intimately, understanding and valuing their differences, lays the foundation and sets the atmosphere for developing an agreeable and strategic financial plan. Deciphering different points of view should produce **light**, not **heat**! The "other side of that coin" —the antithesis— is refusing to value differences, resulting in forfeiture of relational capital. Just as financial portfolios exist, so do emotional portfolios, and they are even more volatile than financial futures. We must learn to value people over things, as does God.

The way couples handle money has great impact on their relationship with God, both individually and corporately. It is interesting that in the Bible, Jesus talks about money more than any other topic! He obviously knew we would have problems in this area. If it was important to him, it ought to be important to us. As we have stated, *money is cited as the number one cause of divorce in our country.* Perhaps the reader is thinking, "Money is not my problem, the **lack** of money is." While it is quite easy to conclude that controlling more capital will solve problems, more often than not an increase in wealth simply *compounds* them. Increased prosperity carries with it increased levels of responsibility and accountability, which take time, that in our busy lives, is in short supply.

> *From everyone who has been given much, much will be demanded; and from the one who has been entrusted with much, much more will be asked.*
> *—Luke 12:48 (NIV)*

God clearly communicates that those with greater assets have an obligation to wisely disperse those resources, since we shall be held accountable to him for our actions. Since everything actually belongs to God and comes from God, we are to function as God's asset managers; we have the same fiduciary responsibility as a broker is required to have with his client.

We believe that many marriages fail not from lack of *desire* to succeed but from the lack of *knowledge.* Just as failure to understand our differences generates friction in marriage, lack of understanding the biblical and practical principles of riches can have the same damaging effect.

In the following chapters we want to assist you in identifying your current financial position and provide you with increased knowledge that will assist you in practical ways to better control your **lifestyle**, **save** what you need to save, **accumulate** the money you will need for the future, and develop a plan that will enable you to **give** from your heart with thanksgiving.

Three Types of Money

To help you accomplish these goals, and for purposes of teaching, let us categorize money into three types, which should make our discussion more meaningful.

Figure 1 represents all the money you will ever earn. The amount of money that will pass through your hands during your lifetime is finite. The amount for which any person will be held accountable varies: some more than others, but we must all give an account for the resources entrusted to us. As we opened the chapter, we quoted Paul's instruction to the church at Corinth:

> *Moreover it is required in stewards, that a man be found faithful.*
> *—1 Corinthians 4:2 (KJV)*

Identifying these three distinct types of money will help to clarify how to handle money, and provide a framework for the remainder of our discussion.

These three varieties of funds are:

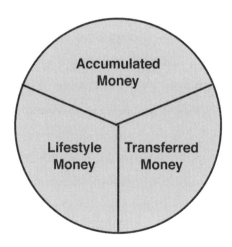

1. **Accumulated Money.** This consists of what we currently have saved and dollars we are saving. Saving is a difficult task at best for most of us, because it directly competes with our lifestyle funds.

Most people think of saving money like dieting. We know we *need* to save, and *want* to save, but it is easier to postpone until later. After years of neglect, we are tempted to take unnecessary risk to make up for our past lack of discipline, much like "crash dieting."

2. **Lifestyle Money**. These are the funds spent to maintain our desired standard of living (house, car, clothing, vacations, etc.). One of the major roadblocks for many of us in managing the other types of money is the cost of maintaining the level of our current lifestyle. Few are willing to decrease their present lifestyle in order to secure their future. A term used during the past couple of decades is "upwardly mobile," not "downwardly mobile!" Getting out of debt usually requires reduction of lifestyle—not an impossibility—but nonetheless difficult. We all know we should be saving more. However, the thought of *reducing* our standard of living never seems to occur to us. Have you ever thought, "I've earned this, I deserve it and I can spend it any way I choose"!? That thought could lead us to impulsive buying, since the goal of modern advertising is to make certain that *something* will always be on your consumer radar.

We would like to introduce you to a new concept in relation to Lifestyle Funds, one that will never get any "press coverage" from Financial Institutions or Advisors. We call it "Lifestyle Ceiling."

Establishing a Lifestyle Ceiling

Did you ever wonder why we assume that our income and lifestyle should automatically escalate over time? The fact that this is faulty reasoning is certainly born out in our faltering economy: bigger and better houses, luxury automobiles, boats, condos on the beach, and much, much more. Now the loans are being called; the bills need to be paid. Who could argue with the fact that financing a high standard of living through consumer credit is foolish? Accumulation for the sake of accumulation is far different than accumulating responsibly for the future. The concept of deferred gratification is now almost unheard of. TV commercials are replete with this sentiment: "I want it, and I want it NOW!"

The objective in life is not to "get all you can, can all you get and sit on the lid." If spouses do not discuss their approach to lifestyle—and answer the question, "How much is enough?"—lack of resolution of differences in the management of the family treasury is certain to create conflict. Tiger Bailey, our rising "now generation" young professional, is trading his future security to build a present image, an illusion with no substance or solid foundation. The safety and security of a home for his wife—bringing her needs into the total equation—did not seem to figure into his thinking. We will address the high cost of Tiger's quest for status in our next chapter.

To establish a lifestyle ceiling, list all your hopes, dreams, needs and other lifestyle expenditures employing a "windfall" mentality: "what if we had unlimited funds?" Then, prayerfully submit each item for God's inspection and approval: insurance, investments, children's education, vacations, automobiles (how many?), housing (how big, what style?) and so on. Once everything has been prioritized according to God's standard for them—unique to each marriage—a ceiling can be identified (not in hard dollars, but subjectively). Effectively, a line will have been drawn: the limits of everything under the line has been agreed upon, and *everything above that ceiling or line is to be committed to God — 100% — with no thought of "making deals" with him.*

Those who have completed this exercise report great joy and freedom in their lives, and because they have turned their focus away from temporal things to the eternal, they find they are able to give generously to the needs of others from whatever amounts exceed the ceiling level of their lifestyle. Since greed is a deadly vice, this practical step is a highly effective weapon to combat it. For the follower of Christ, charitable giving is a command, and therefore should be a vital part of his lifestyle money.

3. **Transferred Money.** This third type of currency is that which you may be losing or *transferring away* unknowingly and unnecessarily. Not every financial decision we make is a good one or one that moves us forward. The fact that there are so many money decisions to make almost guarantees that we will not be as efficient as we might hope with every dollar we spend.

Here is a list of a few areas where potential transfers may occur:
- **Financing Cars**
- **Credit Card Debt**
- **Mortgage Loans**
- **Qualified Retirement Accounts**
- Taxes
- Taxable Savings Accounts
- Mortgage Insurance
- Disability Protection
- Homeowners Insurance
- Major Medical Insurance
- Wills and Trusts
- Term Insurance
- Long Term Care
- College Tuition
- Weddings

In succeeding chapters we will only have time to focus on the four highlighted areas in the above list, but understand that it is possible to transfer money unnecessarily in nearly every financial decision we make. Our level of understanding of these decisions and how they impact us can end up costing us thousands of dollars. Don't forget that if you lose a dollar you did not have to lose, you also lost what that dollar could have earned had you been able to retain it (opportunity cost).

We ask again the key question of this book: *If what you thought to be true turned out not to be true, when would you want to know?* Our tendency is to assume we know all we need to know about money, but unfortunately, that can be a costly error. No one ever wakes up in the morning thinking, "I know what I am doing financially is wrong, but I'm stickin' to it." We believe that we are doing is right!

Think again about where you gained your knowledge about money. We said earlier that we all begin by emulating family members and friends, gradually adding and deleting from our financial data bank as we are exposed to a variety of other sources. Usually, our failures become our greatest teacher.

There is more to be gained in avoiding financial losses than in picking winners. Obviously, once this crucial concept is understood, it makes good sense to employ this principal of avoiding unnecessary transfers in every financial decision we face, especially in light of the fact that we are responsible for **God's** assets!

Ways to Enhance Your Financial Position

There are only three ways to increase or enhance your financial position:

1. Save more.
2. Increase rate of return.
3. Increase efficiency.

As we have said, the first—saving—is difficult and requires discipline, the second involves risk, *but the third option can move us forward with dollars we are presently losing unknowingly and unnecessarily.*

It is certainly true that higher returns and better investments can increase a person's net worth, but to focus solely on rate of return may not always produce optimal results. As we have said, greater impact is actually found in avoiding losses rather than picking winners. That does not mean that you should avoid investments that pay higher returns. However, to make high returns the sole *focus* can be detrimental—requiring unnecessary risk. Those who crave riches are warned about the outcome:

> But those who desire to be rich fall into temptation, into a snare, into many senseless and harmful desires that plunge people into ruin and destruction. For the love of money is a root of all kinds of evils. It is through this craving that some have wandered away from the faith and pierced themselves with many pangs.
> —1 Timothy 6:9-10 (ESV)

To improve our current financial position, we may naturally assume that we will have to cut back or give up something. Unfortunately, for many people the thought of imposing restraints today in order to improve the future is so stressful that it keeps them from taking any action at all.

There are few books on financial dieting. A few authors have attempted to teach principles of budget control and planning. But, not only is it unpopular, most of the systems they advocate are even more difficult to sustain than going on a physical diet. Food appetites come and go, but our appetite for money is insatiable. If expense and lifestyle reduction is not an option for you, you will be tempted to search for investments claiming to pay higher returns and assume more risk than is prudent.

As an illustration, let's use a golf analogy. Searching for the best investments with the highest returns is the equivalent of buying new clubs to improve your game. While it is important to have good clubs and it is possible to improve your game with better equipment, the greater impact will come from *perfecting your swing.* Finding a better club to hit the ball further (increased rate of return) can be advantageous. However, hitting the ball a greater distance can also bring with it disadvantages (increased risk). Without a higher level of skill, your accuracy will be unpredictable.

If you were invited to play in The Masters Tournament, golf's most prestigious event, would you choose to have the better clubs (equipment) of a great player or his world-class abilities? Obviously, you would want his **ability** (his swing).

What do financial institutions deliver? **Clubs** or **swings?** They have <u>products</u> to sell, which we will call the <u>clubs</u>. Everyone needs clubs to play, but having the correct <u>swing</u> is much more valuable. This is what we call efficiency or effectiveness: having the flawless financial swing means that you have avoided unnecessary wealth transfers, thereby making your money perform at its maximum potential: ***making it do all it can do.*** You should focus on *accuracy* before *distance.* The best place to start is to eliminate unnecessary transfers before searching for better investments. *Get your "financial swing" correct before you look for new clubs.*

Understanding Your Financial Bucket

If you are going to avoid losses in your financial life, you will first need to know where those loses may occur. We will look at a few areas together that could change your outlook on money for the rest of your life. Consider this: there are two ways to fill a bucket with holes in it.

- The first is to pour more into it.
- The second is to plug the holes first. The bucket will now fill even if the flow is just a trickle.

Which one of these two strategies have the financial institutions suggested you employ in your current financial position? Have they been helping you plug the holes or simply telling you to pour more in?

So, how do you plug the holes in your financial bucket? *By avoiding unnecessary transfers.* The exciting thing is that by avoiding them, dollars are then freed up for you to put towards future savings, present lifestyle, or giving. What if you could **save more** without having to take those dollars from your current lifestyle accounts, which are already strained? What if there were more dollars available for you to recapture from what you are currently losing? Most people will lose more getting where they are going than they will have when they get there!

Or, what if you could **give** more simply by avoiding losses? Christian believers are exhorted in Scripture to give toward building God's kingdom and not their own.

> But seek first the kingdom of God and his righteousness,
> and all these things will be added to you.
> —Matthew 6:33 (ESV)

As we have said, giving is to be a major concern for followers of Christ. We may become highly educated and proficient money managers, but without adherence to God's principles of wealth management, we can expect no blessing from God on our financial affairs.

When you evaluate your financial life, comparing actual vs. opportunity costs, you will eventually discover there are potentially hundreds of thousands of dollars slipping through your fingers during your lifetime. If you were able to recapture some of that lost opportunity money, it could make a considerable difference in your ability to provide for your family, give with a grateful heart and honor God with your resources.

Even the Scriptures speak of opportunity costs:

> *Give away your life; you'll find life given back, but not merely*
> *given back—given back with bonus and blessing. Giving, not*
> *getting, is the way. Generosity begets generosity.*
> *—Luke 6:38 (The Message)*

You may be surprised if we said that you probably make enough money. God only promises to meet your **needs**. How *much* you make is not as important as what you do with what you have been given. God's standard is always "faithfulness to opportunity." The overriding theme is that you must begin to look at money not just in relation to what it can do for you today but also what it can do for you and others in the future.

The Bible speaks of the "Law of the Harvest": If you do not plant you will see no crop. Getting our current lifestyle under control is a critical part of us being able to put away the money we will require in our later years. In the following chapters, we will begin to address specific areas that are potential financial pitfalls.

Exactly where are you giving away money? What are those lost opportunities? We have some major areas of life to look at. You will be amazed at how much money you are giving away unknowingly and unnecessarily. Unknowingly means you are forgiven: you did not know. Unnecessarily means you can fix it.

Let's get to work.

Chapter 10

The High Cost of Status

Then the cares and anxieties of the world and distractions of the age, and the pleasure and delight and false glamour and deceitfulness of riches, and the craving and passionate desire for other things creep in and choke and suffocate the Word, and it becomes fruitless.
—Mark 4:19 (Amplified Bible)

The last time we peered in on our friends the Baileys, in Chapter 6, Tiger had just received a raise, and finally realized he had to do something about servicing the substantive debt that the two of them had accumulated since their wedding. He actually devised a plan, arranged a romantic rendezvous at Kitty's favorite restaurant, and unveiled the details as to the use of the increased revenue. His young bride, Kitty, still dreaming idealistically about a bungalow in the suburbs, was unimpressed with his proposition. Instead of using the money to buy a house, Tiger chose to focus on debt reduction and regular savings toward a down payment on that new home.

Seemed like a savvy strategy, right? We applauded Tiger's sudden taming of his impulsive tendencies. He moved from focusing solely on NOW and turned his attention toward LATER. His previous pattern had been spending without consideration of any future consequence.

Months have now passed. Stuffing his good intensions in his hip pocket, Tiger is once again up to his old tricks! His "financial diet"—curbing consumer cravings—lasted about as long as last year's New Year's resolution. He's hungry, but not for physical food. His out-of-debt strategy didn't even last until Christmas! With debt elimination finally in sight, he dropped his binoculars!

"Boys like their toys," or so the saying goes. Men seem to have an inordinate fascination with planes, trains and automobiles. Suddenly, Tiger's NOW-LATER plan has undergone a metamorphosis to NOW-NOW, or we might say, NOW-WOW! You can guess the source: the lure of a brand spanking new vehicle—shiny, sleek, and fashionable—a foreign luxury car!

"I'll be the envy of the neighbors," he was thinking as he once again fought traffic through winter weather, speeding unknowingly toward another caustic confrontation. He is about to negate everything he has gained, and the trust he has slowly begun to build, by reneging on his commitment to Kitty. In an irresponsible stroke of a pen he inked a new contract for 72 months that could cancel a vow he made forever.

His desire to appear successful has once again surfaced, and threatens to further weaken, if not destroy, the very foundation of his finances and his marriage.

The origin of this present predicament: a $5000 Christmas bonus. Without consulting Kitty, he plunked down half of it for the down payment on the car of his dreams. His rationale? He put the *other* half in their future home down payment savings account, thinking that would appease her and win approval of his latest selfish desire (a perfect example of two *living as two not one).*

Picture this: he is on his way home from the dealer, after signing a contract on his new wheels, actually thinking Kitty will be impressed! It doesn't take a rocket scientist to predict the outcome of this decision!

On the way home Tiger called Kitty to invite her out to dinner, thinking, of course, that he would surprise her, and that she would naturally share his enthusiasm. Nothing could have been further from the truth. Bursting with excitement as he flung open the apartment door, he looked back one more time at his prize, prominently displayed for the entire neighborhood to see.

"Honey, I'm home! Come on outside; I've got something to show you!" He ushered her to the door, expecting her to be overjoyed with his purchase. Instead, an obvious look of disbelief spread over her face.

"You bought this without telling me? What happened to our plans for a house? I thought we were saving for a down payment. How could you do this to me? Tiger, sometimes I just don't understand you!" Kitty's face flushed, and tears began to well up in her eyes.

"Before you say anything else, I did put some money in the house account."

"Some of what? Where did you get the money?"

"I got a Christmas bonus—$5,000. I've dreamed of owning a car like this my whole life. I finally got a chance to get it and I took it."

"I, what about We…" And what about kids? You know I have been wanting to start our family."

"It's always what *you* want isn't it?"

"What *I* want? Tiger, as long as we have been married, you have controlled the money, and you always seem to make sure you get what **you** want. I don't know how much longer I can take this." Kitty, exasperated and angry, announced, "I'm not interested in dinner, and I sure don't want to go anywhere in your new car!"

"Fine." Frustrated, and with arms thrown in the air, Tiger stormed out of the door, seeking sanctuary in the comfort of his new vehicle, which had suddenly lost that "new car smell." Oblivious to the fact that he has become a captive of commerce, he sped away, not even knowing where he was going. You could hear the tires and tailpipes echo in the distance, the fading noise paralleling their fading marriage.

Kitty began to compose herself, realizing she would probably spend the night alone. She wasn't sure she cared if Tiger came back. She just needed time to think.

While driving aimlessly around town, Tiger called Tim, his "free-again" recently-divorced sports buddy, looking for some sympathy. Explaining the situation in a decidedly biased way, he related to him that Kitty "just doesn't get it," and that he felt it was time to bolt out of his marriage.

"Its over," he thought to himself as he drove toward Tim's house to crash on his sofa. "Some early Christmas present."

The Truth About Transferred Money

At the core of the incident related above is an issue that is the cause of many misunderstandings in marriage: purchasing and financing automobiles. Tiger and Kitty are simply fictional characters that make the same mistakes WE do. The car debacle is simply the culmination of a number of problems that have been piling up in their relationship, and now an **automobile** is about to level the landscape of their lives.

Financing cars is probably the one area where more money is lost than any other financial decision you will ever make. We said in our last chapter that a major key to wealth accumulation is the eradication or reduction of transferred money—that is, interest paid to others. It is a sad but true fact that Americans *may lose more money financing the vehicles that **get** them to work, than they will accumulate in their lifelong savings accounts **at** work*

If couples are going to solve their money problems they must understand the principle of lost opportunity cost and the two most common areas losses occurs are—automobile financing and credit card debt. The Bailey's problems might have been lessened had they better understood how to handle their assets in these two areas.

Let's look more closely at financing cars, a major expense we will incur many times throughout our lives.

The Devastating Impact of Financing Cars

Few understand the full impact that transferring interest in the form of finance payments on vehicles has on their lives. Most of us understand that paying non-deductible interest is not a winning strategy, but we often view it as a necessary evil. Over a lifetime the interest paid on financing automobiles, plus the opportunity cost forfeited by doing this, *may account for one of our biggest financial blunders. How* to pay for your cars is the salient issue.

The answer lies not in **what** you buy, but **how** you buy it. In **every** financial decision you must not only consider the price of the item, but you must also factor in the opportunity cost of the purchase. Opportunity cost is the hidden component in the equation. Getting around in that nice car of yours can cost more than you realize!

You see, what you pay for the cost of the automobile is only **one** cost; what you could have **earned** had you not relinquished the interest is the opportunity cost. Few buyers will ever get this kind of information from a car dealer. You may not be able to solve this problem on the car you presently own, but consider those vehicles you will purchase in the future.

One solution to this dilemma is to create an account that will allow you to withdraw the money necessary to pay **cash** for your next car and then **pay yourself back**—not only the principal, but also the interest you would have paid the lending institution. We will address this more momentarily, but first let's turn our attention to the matter of credit cards.

The Equally Devastating Impact
of Credit Card Debt

If you were to examine the Bailey treasury, the car purchase was only the tip of the iceberg. Tiger had kept other monetary matters from Kitty. Since he handled all the finances, and she had never looked at their credit score, she was unaware that he was carrying a $10,000 balance on a credit card. Tiger heedlessly had the statements sent to his office. Ostensibly, he had planned to use the card only for business, but found himself increasingly using it to support his fantasy of success and status.

One day Kitty discovered one of thee credit card statements that Tiger had left in his coat pocket, and confronted him.

"What's this?" she demanded.

"It's business—*my* business," was his lame excuse. Unable to articulate a palpable reason for his actions, he made a feeble attempt to justify himself.

"I earned the money and I think I should be able to spend it any way I choose." (It had always been his plan to pay it off with a future bonus, but he always found something else to spend the money on—the latest thing being the car.)

Tiger simply did not understand the impact his decision to finance the car, as well as his credit card debt (added to the other credit cards and school loans), was having on his marriage and their overall financial health. He was pouring his money into a bucket with holes in it!

The wisest and richest man who ever lived—Solomon—gave some insights on the subject of money many centuries ago. These timeless truths are as applicable today as they have been down through the ages, and, if understood and applied could spare each of us much grief.

Heed these ancient Hebrew Proverbs:

> ...*for riches do not endure forever, and a crown is not secure for all generations.*
> —*Proverbs 27:24*

> *Better a poor man whose walk is blameless than a rich man whose ways are perverse.*
> —*Proverbs 28:6*

> *A rich man may be wise in his own eyes, but a poor man who has discernment sees through him.*
> — *Proverbs 28:11*

> *A stingy man is eager to get rich and is unaware that poverty awaits him.*
> — *Proverbs 28:22*

> ...*give me neither poverty nor riches, but give me only my daily bread. Otherwise, I may have too much and disown you and say, 'Who is the Lord?' Or I may become poor and steal, and so dishonor the name of my God.*
> — *Proverbs 30:8-9*

The "Bottom Line" on the Subject of Credit Cards

There is really only one thing to say about credit cards—Pay them off in full every month and never make a late payment.

Credit cards are a convenient and necessary part of life in the world in which we live. However, any *interest* you pay on credit cards is diminishing the interest you could be earning on investment accounts. On the surface credit cards do not appear to cause undue hardship, but over a lifetime mishandling them can cause financial devastation.

It makes little sense to pay interest to others, and at the same time take risk trying to earn interest on money invested. If you are driving to work in a car that has been financed, and you have credit card debt—even though you are putting money away for your retirement—you are in "financial neutral." You **must** solve this problem.

To underscore the central theme of this chapter: the **cost** is not only the interest you **pay** but the **opportunity cost** of what the interest would have **earned** had you not transferred it away. Credit card debt creates a wealth transfer, and one that must be avoided if you are to maximize your wealth potential and improve your family's financial health. The number one reason given for divorce in our country is money. Money is not the problem itself, but rather the **issues** that surface from the lack of understanding of how money functions.

To gain a better understanding of this, here are some secrets the banks are not telling you.

The Most Powerful Bank in the World

What is the most powerful bank in the world? Let's begin by setting the stage for the kind of bank we are talking about: it's **not** about global banking institutions, or how to set up a charter to open a local bank like the one in your neighborhood. What we are alluding to could change the way you look at banking and your money for the rest of your life!

The most powerful bank in the world is "**Your Bank**."

There are some important lessons to learn from traditional banks and how they earn money that you would do well to incorporate into this new type of bank. You see, "Your Bank" refers more to a *financial position* than to the brick and mortar building where you conduct your conventional banking. "Your Bank" is simply an **account** that you set up, which has liquid assets over which you have control. From this point on we will refer to this account as "Your Bank."

Although many consider them similar, there is a difference between *banking* and *investing*; however, both have earning capital as their primary objective. Note first how a traditional bank acquires and grows its assets.

A bank must first attract customers and persuade them to deposit funds in their institution. They do not create **products** to attract depositors; they provide **services** to attract customers. One such service is free checking accounts. They charge no fee for this service in order to gain access to a depositor's money.

Banks must also make it convenient for clients to do business with them, so they extend teller hours, provide online banking and direct deposits for patrons' paychecks. They pay **interest** to convince people to put additional money in their bank. The more money that is deposited in their institution, the higher the interest rate they are able to pay out. The longer customers leave their funds in a bank the more benefits and services they enjoy.

Banking institutions also encourage customers to retain their funds with them long term, and usually impose penalties for early withdrawals. As further incentive to leave money on deposit, they may offer higher interest rates on funds left over longer time periods. Banks charge more interest than they pay out by providing a "spread," which covers the cost of operations and hopefully produces a profit.

Reflect on this: how do banks advise people to make money? Their number one recommendation is that a client deposit his money, not withdraw it, and simply watch the "magic" of compound interest do its thing. Interestingly, *that is not what they do; they keep the money moving—they take it in and loan it out to someone else.*

The purpose of this review of banking practices is to encourage you to begin to think about how you can apply some of their wealth accumulation principals to "Your Bank." Remember: you will either be a **customer** of a bank or you will learn how to **be the bank**.

Banks make loans to some people because they have the ability to repay those loans over time. However, most loans require *collateral.* Most often, when people take out loans at a bank, they also have money in other accounts, such as retirement funds or home equity. Usually, those monies are inaccessible, so people are forced to borrow.

Herein lies a problem: the interest a consumer pays to borrow money offsets the return they are earning on money they have invested. There is a hidden cost to borrowing. If you pay a dollar in interest that you could have avoided, you are not only losing that dollar, but you are also losing what that dollar could have earned for you had you not given it away. That is another illustration of opportunity cost.

Let's dig deeper. Suppose you carried a $10,000 credit card balance at 18%. You would have to pay the bank $1,972 in interest over the year. Doing the same thing over 40 years of your lifetime would result in you losing almost $78,866 in interest. That's a lot of money— but that's not all of it.

You did not lose just the interest. You **also** lost the *opportunity to invest* $1,972 each year. Had you not paid that interest, but instead invested it in "Your Bank" and averaged 6% a year earnings, you would have about $305,135 in 40 years! If you averaged 8% you would have almost $510,767!

Traditional banks fully understand the power of this principal— which is why the banking industry is so profitable. You either **pay** interest or **earn** interest; there is no in between.

The question again, is: "Would you like to be a **customer** of a bank or would you like to **be** the bank?"

Assuming you are interested in setting up "Your Bank," you are obviously going to have to accumulate some cash. First, you must find a place to put the money, which will then allow you to operate like a bank and also provide you some additional benefits.

Willy Sutton (1901-1980) was one of the most famous bank robbers of the twentieth century. It is estimated that he robbed over

100 banks of over $2 million in his lifetime. Sutton is famously (and probably falsely) known for answering a reporter, Mitch Ohnstad, who asked why he robbed banks by saying, *"because that's where the money is."* [1] (Some have quoted Willy as saying, "that's where they keep the money.")

How will you protect your money from the Willy Suttons of today? You could be your own worst enemy. In your search for the right type of account to "keep your money," here is a list of benefits you will want to make sure the account provides.

- The money must be safe, with no chance of loss
- The money in the account should grow tax deferred
- When you withdraw funds they should be tax free
- The account should pay a competitive rate of return
- The interest you earn must be guaranteed
- The money in the account should be safe from creditors
- There ought to be no deposit limits
- There should be no restrictions on how you can use the money
- You may use the value of the account as collateral
- You have total liquidity, use, and control
- In the event of a disability your money should still be accessible
- The value of the account should never go down

The good news is that there are several types of accounts that will allow you to "be your own bank." However, some of them are more efficient than others. Some provide potential for higher returns but do not function well as a bank. Others perform well as a bank but offer little or no return and few benefits.

While exploring options for "Your Bank" you should consult a qualified financial services professional to discuss the particular financial products ("clubs" in our previous golf analogy) that provide the most benefits and best rates of return. Most people keep very little money in local banks, and savings are most often found in qualified retirement plans (401k, IRA, SEP, 403B) or home equity. While these may be great accounts to **accumulate** money, they do not function well as a bank because they do not offer liquidity.

If you are forced to borrow money because you don't have access to **your** money, the interest you are losing is reducing the rate of return on your invested dollars (lost opportunity cost).

Let's look at a very common example. Many people put money into a qualified retirement account at work, which is not necessarily a bad thing, especially if there is a company match. But because they do not have access to this money they may be forced to finance the car they need to get to work. We are not saying you should not have a car. You simply need a better way to pay for it.

It's easy to see that if you are saving money and earning 6% interest, but you are paying 6% on borrowed money, the effect is you are not moving at all. The interest you pay on borrowed money should demand at least as much attention—if not more—than the interest you are earning, because it is something you can avoid.

Earning interest requires risk; avoiding loss of interest reduces risk. As we have pointed out, avoiding losses can prove more valuable than picking winners with higher returns.

Another way to look at this is that you should not only look at how much you have, but you should also know how much it cost you to get it. Unfortunately, many people focus all of their attention on saving and investing with little consideration given to borrowed funds. For example, let's assume that you have $30,000 in the bank earning 4%. If you were to buy a $30,000 car and finance it at 6% you would be losing money!

Further, if your $30,000 earning 4% was in a taxable account it would yield even less because the interest earned is *taxable*.

Obviously, a bank could not pay out 6% while earning only 4% —and neither should **you**! *You need to look at what you are giving away in interest, not just the interest you are earning.*

Suppose you withdrew $30,000 from "Your Bank" and paid cash for the car. You could probably get a better deal. Now suppose you paid yourself back using the same car payment you would have paid, at the same 6% interest rate the car dealer was going to charge you had you financed it. At the end of the loan period, you would have not only the $30,000, but the interest you would have given the lending institution as well. That is what it means to be your own bank.

We actually finance everything we purchase. We either **pay** interest or **earn** interest. Even if we pay cash we are financing, because we have to consider what the money would have earned had we kept it—we lost the opportunity to use the money in some other fashion. What if you could totally avoid paying interest and **redirect** all the interest you are currently paying into "Your Bank"? That is the way a bank thinks!

You may be saying to yourself, "This all sounds very good, but where am I going to come up with the money to get my bank started?" That is actually a great question. Like most things of value, it will take some time to get "Your Bank" up and running, but the payoff is worth the effort.

You may be surprised to discover that the money you need to get "Your Bank" started can often be found in areas of your financial affairs where you are losing unknowingly and unnecessarily, without any real impact on your current lifestyle. Common areas include how you pay for your home, taxes, how you finance your cars, credit card purchases, and how you intend to send your children to college, just to name a few.

Think about this: who won the first time you played the game tick-tack-toe? Of course! It was the person who taught you the game. They said, "I am the X and you are the O, the object is to get three in a row." We all lost regularly until we learned the strategies of the game.

The same is true in the world of finance. The financial institutions that you and I have to deal with on a daily basis have rules. Do they teach you the rules? Of course not. You must learn the rules as you play; unfortunately, you can lose a great deal of money in the process.

We suggest that you get started today building The Most Powerful Bank In The World. In our efforts to wisely manage the resources God has given into our hands, we would do well to understand the ancient prophet who reminds us of this:

> Thus says the Lord: "Let not the wise man glory in his wisdom, Let not the mighty man glory in his might, Nor let the rich man glory in his riches; But let him who glories glory in this, That he understands and knows Me, That I am the Lord, exercising lovingkindness, judgment, and righteousness in the earth. For in these I delight," says the Lord.
> — Jeremiah 9:23,24 (NKJ)

It's not so much the amount of money you amass during your lifetime, as it is what you DO with the money God gives you. Jesus, in Luke 2:52, was described as having increased in "wisdom, stature, favor with God and favor with men."

Sorting out the various dimensions of life helps keep us in balance:

- ❧ Wisdom: mental
- ❧ Stature: physical
- ❧ Favor with God: spiritual
- ❧ Favor with men: social or relational

It will take a great deal of mental focus in our microwave age to develop the level of expertise you will need to apply right financial principles, exercise the patience required to manage your portfolio, defer personal gratification and yet give generously to God's kingdom.

The phrase, "favor with God" points to the importance of the spiritual aspect of life. Tiger Baileys ambition led him to an untenable trap. He has fallen victim to the age-old vices of arrogance and greed. He desperately needs help, for he seems to have totally removed God from the equation of his marriage, his job, and his finances. Be careful not to throw stones before examining your own life!

We have underscored the need to plug up the holes in our financial buckets by learning how to avoid transferring wealth away in the form of interest payments, and the importance of saving so that we might become our own bank. In a subsequent chapter, we will look more closely at saving opportunities.

In our next chapter we will turn our attention to the largest purchase you probably will ever make in your life—a home. You might be surprised to find out that how you pay for your home can make a huge difference in your financial future. If what you thought to be true about buying your home turned out not to be true, when would you want to know?

What you DON'T know may be more important than what you DO know!

Chapter 11

The Mystery of Mortgages

Jesus replied, "Foxes have holes and birds of the air have nests, but the Son of Man has no place to lay his head."
— *Luke 9:58 (NIV)*

But if we have food and clothing, we will be content with that.
— *1 Timothy 6:8 (NIV)*

Stu Stuckey had always considered himself an island of reason in a sea of passion: two teenage daughters and a wonderful, highly energetic wife whom he felt to be less effective in dealing with money matters. For all the years of their marriage Stu had managed the family funds, and Dina, though sometimes included in discussions, was far less "in the loop" than she desired.

One of the elements of Stu's carefully plotted financial plan was his schedule to pay off their house—the "great American dream." He set an evening aside to break the great news to Dina that he had the final payment in hand to pay off their mortgage. His autocratic control of the family budget (much to Dina's displeasure) had enabled him to make extra principle payments without her knowledge or consent.

As we catch up with the Stuckey family, Stu and Dina are seated in an up-scale restaurant—a touch of panache for a usually conservative financial manager! After ordering their meals, and with a sudden euphoric sense of possibility, Stu announced, "Dina, I have some great news. I have been able to manage our finances well enough that we are able to pay off the mortgage this month!"

Somewhat mystified, Dina responded, "I don't understand. How is that possible? I thought we had fifteen years yet before our house was paid off?"

"Well, I just got another raise... I guess the company is still pleased with my work! And that, along with the extra payments I have been making, will enable me to pay off the house much earlier than I had originally planned. Look—here's the check."

"Are you kidding me? I think that's about the greatest news I have heard in years!"

If you will remember our previous glimpses of conversations and family interactions in the Stuckey household, and the disposition of our charming "shop-'til-you-drop" travel-agent working mom, you can only imagine the ideas that are now firing in rapid succession in her brain! Blend Dina's aspirations with Stu's spreadsheet mentality and you can only imagine the massive misunderstanding which is about to unfold.

Unable to contain her excitement, Dina optimistically added, "Does this mean I can finally move ahead with the convertible we discussed and put on hold? And I can't wait to get started on the kitchen remodeling you wouldn't even discuss with me. There are tons of other things we need to do to our house to update it, Stu."

Stu, rather than provoke public embarrassment, quietly excused himself to the rest room to "stew" for a moment. When he returned to the table, outwardly rational and cautious, he struggled to orchestrate a dialogue to steer the course of the conversation comfortably enough so as not to ruin the mood he had worked so hard to create.

Stu sat down and took a deep breath before speaking. "Honey, I think we need to slow down a little here, and think this through.

Don't lose sight of the fact that we have two children to send through college, and our own retirement years to think about. You want our 'golden years' to be golden, don't you?"

Already sensing the cauldron of contention brewing just by looking at Dina's face, Stu added condescendingly, "I have made plans to meet with our financial planner this Friday to discuss the best options as we move forward on this."

Push the pause button; you can imagine the next scene. Their meal was over before it was even served! Silence in the sanctuary of matrimony: transmitter and receiver buttons have both been muted. Stu wasted a lot of his well-managed bucks for that bust!

What happened? Dina's initial excitement rapidly turned to despair. Here, two polar opposites are trying to carry on a conversation in a vacuum; the incident had a predictable outcome. In Dina's mind, she had waited so long for so many things. *Waiting* was always Stu's end game. There never seemed to be a "now" in his vocabulary; it was always "later" on his time line. She had no sense of being held in esteem, and she did not feel Stu valued her opinion. He rarely consulted her on money issues, and now, faced with an extremely critical decision, he did not even *include* her; in fact, he had been HIDING making extra principal payments from her!

Dina felt somewhat deceived. She had been doing without for so long without really knowing why; and now that she knew why, she wasn't sure she liked it!

Stu, on the other hand, felt totally justified in his actions. Committed, careful, consistent and persistent in his personal and professional life, he did what he felt was right for his family. Stu and Dina again are faced with the continuing saga of misunderstanding their Divine Design, and in this case a major monetary misunderstanding again brought on a serious confrontation and disagreement.

As we continue in the vein of practical teaching on finance in Part 2 of this volume, let's review our progress: we first wrestled with the dangers of wealth and riches, then examined the various types of money. Next we were shocked as we checked out the high cost of status! We are ready now to address a crucial concept—how to finance our family residences. This one is fraught with divergent opinions.

Stu's actions were based on *what he believed to be true about mortgages, but which might not be true at all.* Where had he gleaned his information? Just because we have heard something from so-called "experts," been trained on it in a seminar or read it in a book does not mean it is accurate. Data surrounding the financing of homes can truly be a mystery! In this chapter, we hope to de-mystify the mortgage matter for you, to help you make better decisions, improve the quality of your marriage and possibly avoid a "Stu and Dina Stuckey conversation" such as we have witnessed above.

When you look at all the different mortgage options available among lending institutions, choosing the right one can be daunting, and **the choice you make will depend on what you think is true about mortgages and what is not.**

Mortgages: the Right Choice

To get started we would like you to take the following simple True or False quiz.

1. T___F___ A large down payment will save you more money on your mortgage over time than a small down payment

2. T___F__ A 15-year mortgage will save more money over time than a 30-year mortgage

3. T___F__ Making extra principle payments saves you money

4. T___F___ The interest rate is the main factor in determining the cost of a mortgage

5. T___F___ You are more secure having your home paid off than financed 100%

If what you thought to be true turned out not to be true, when would you want to know?

To facilitate our understanding of an otherwise complex concept, we will employ the services of three fictitious couples—friends of the Stuckeys and Baileys—to examine a few things about mortgages that could change how you view and handle your money for the rest of your life. Our new friends are:

- 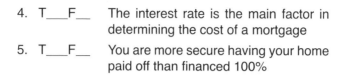 **The Free-n-Clears**
- **The Owe-it-Alls**
- **The Pay-Extras**

Each of these "couples" represents an approach to handling a mortgage that is widely held by a particular group of homeowners. And any or all of these views are potential "what if what you believed to be true turned out not to be true" lines of reasoning. We'll take the quiz again later to see if your thinking changes.

The first couple, **The Free-n-Clears,** epitomize those who have their homes paid off completely, with no mortgage and no additional debt. Even if you currently are not in this position, you may have found yourself in the past thinking this is where you want to be. After all, having your home paid for is still held out to be an American dream.

Our second couple is the **Owe-it-alls**. They have the money and could pay cash for their home, but have decided to keep their money and invest it in a safe place, requiring them to make monthly mortgage payments. They, too, have no other debt.

We understand that most readers do not fit in either of these categories, since they represent two extremes. Most homeowners are somewhere in between. The purpose of this chapter is to familiarize you with several other methods to pay off a home! We want to help you determine which might be best for you. As we review the issues surrounding the mortgage model, we will look in on our couples from time to time to gain a better understanding of the principal being illustrated.

Reasons to Carry a Mortgage

To begin with, there are really only three financial reasons to carry a mortgage:

1. **The first is that you do not have enough money to buy a home, so you must borrow the funds.** Most people find ourselves in this camp, so we work diligently to rid ourselves of our mortgage obligation as quickly as possible.

2. **The second reason is the mortgage interest deduction.** There are those who do not itemize their taxes; thus, the deduction is of no value. Others live in homes valued over $1,000,000, and because of their income level the deduction is *phased*. **Question**: If you were to qualify for mortgage interest deductions, how much tax relief would you want until you got your home paid off? **Answer**: All you could get.

3. **The third reason is the spread.** Spread is the difference between what you have to pay to use someone else's money and what you can earn on your own.

Let's look first at the **Free-n-Clears,** who paid cash for their home. They receive no tax deductions, and the money they put in their home is earning zero. They do not *send* a check to the bank, but they also do not *get* a check each month from the bank on the investment they have made in their home.

Conversely, the **Owe-it-Alls** had enough money to pay cash for their home, but decided to keep it and invest it in a safe place where they would have liquidity, use and control of the funds (review the benefits of "Your Bank" listed in chapter 10). They are earning *interest* on their money, and after factoring in the mortgage interest deduction their mortgage payment is less than the interest they are earning. Because they are their own bank, they have the opportunity to earn a *spread* on the money if and when an opportunity comes along that is within their risk tolerance. As we have defined spread, this means this will allow them to earn more interest than they have to pay the mortgage company. They only invest in things they trust and understand.

The **Free-n-Clears** also have investment opportunities, now that they no longer make monthly mortgage payments, but their investment amounts are limited because they do not have access to the larger sum that is now tied up in their home. They will have to assume more risk than the **Owe-it-Alls** if they cannot find a tax-deductible account in which to deposit their after-tax dollars.

The Impact of Inflation

One area people often fail to consider when financing is inflation. This is a basic financial concept but the application can be tricky. If you have a fixed payment today of $2,000 a month, you need to estimate what that same $2,000 would buy in 10, 20 or 30 years to get a clear understanding of your position.

For example, if we assume an inflation rate of 3%, $2,000 will only buy $823.97 worth of goods in 30 years. How does that relate to a mortgage? By prepaying a fixed mortgage early, *we are actually giving the lending institution the most valuable dollars we will ever receive.* That $2,000 today is worth $2,000. *But $2,000 in 30 years will only be worth $823.* Paying a fixed payment will cost you less and less over time due to the reducing purchasing power of a dollar adjusted for inflation.

If you finance you transfer interest to the lending institution for the privilege of using their money. If you pay cash you save interest, but you lose interest as well, because that money is not earning anything for you.

You can see then, that the **Free-N-Clears** invested the most valuable dollars they will ever have in their home. The **Owe-it-Alls** have a fixed payment that allows them to give the bank payments that are worth less and less each month, while keeping their money invested with the potential to offset the impact of inflation.

Think about this. The equity you have in your home today earns zero, and is being eroded further every day by inflation. Let's assume inflation is 3% and your home is appreciating at 3%. If your home was mortgage free and valued today at $100,000, in 15 years that $100,000 will have a purchasing power of only $64,186. Hopefully, your home will *appreciate,* but to fully understand the impact of inflation, let's assume for a moment that your home does *not* appreciate. (Meaning you bought it for $100,000 and will sell it for $100,000 15 years later.)

To purchase a new home of the same value, you would have to pay $135,814 because of the erosion effect of inflation.

Next let's assume your home *did* appreciate at the rate of inflation. If you were to sell your home for $135,000 and start shopping for a new home you will be surprised to find that houses in the $135,000 range are no better than the one you just sold that you paid $100,000 for 15 years ago!

Inflation erodes the purchasing power of your money. Appreciation refers to the value of your asset. Your home must appreciate at the same rate as inflation to remain even.

How Much Should I Put Down?

With that in mind, do the **Free-n-Clears** earn any interest on their down payment? No. Is their down payment accessible? No. But what would their down payment be worth today had they been able to retain and invest it? This opportunity cost is of primary concern.

So let's look at the opportunity cost on that down payment and sharpen our pencils as we take a deeper look. The answer to this question will tell you how much you should put down when you buy a home. The largest down payment one can make on a $300,000 home is how much? Correct: $300,000 if you are the **Free-n-Clears**. Most people obviously cannot pay cash for their home, but many would if they were able. Since most people do not have enough in a lump sum to purchase their home, they are more likely to pay it off a little each month by *accelerating their principal payments*—the **Pay-Extras.** We will investigate this strategy momentarily.

If we consider an investment rate of 8% over a 30-year period, that same down payment of $300,000 would earn $2,980,719 in interest, for a total of $3,280,719! The **Owe-it-Alls** understood this concept, and that is precisely why they kept their money, invested it in "Their Bank," and borrowed from a traditional bank to purchase their home. If the money invested could one day be worth $3,280,719, the question is, "What would that $300,000 house be worth in 30 years?" If it's not worth $3.2 million, you have made a minor financial miscalculation!

Perhaps it has occurred to you that the **Free-n-Clears** have the cash flow to invest since they have no mortgage. That is true; however, *the money they save and invest now uses after-tax dollars* and is _not deductible_. The **Owe-it-Alls** are investing their money and make monthly mortgage payments that _are deductible_. They have calculated that after factoring in the cost of their mortgage loan minus the interest deduction on their taxes, there is likelihood they will come out ahead even if their investments perform only modestly. More importantly, _they maintain control of the money._

The question before us is still: "how much should I put down when I purchase a home?" Remember, your down payment earns zero interest. If your home is paid off, you do not have to pay interest, but you do not earn interest either. And don't forget what inflation is doing to that money.

How long does your down payment stay in a down payment status? _Forever._ On a $300,000 home the required down payment would be $60,000, or 20%. That $60,000, compounded at 8% over 30 years would grow to over $603,000. Think about that! The bank is willing to loan you money for your house, and the down payment you pay them would cover the cost of building the two houses on either side of you!

If you want to pay off your home, it makes more sense for you to keep saving money in "Your Bank" until you have enough to write _one check_ to pay the house off completely, rather than a little each month (as in the form of extra principle payments). _This would allow you to maximize the tax deductions you have available until you decide to pay it off._ This would even help you pay it off faster because as you make principal payments you reduce your deductions, which in turn requires more after tax income to make the future mortgage payments.

Making no down payment would be desirable, but the lending institutions always require collateral. Think through this issue carefully before you make a decision, since regaining control of your money once you have given it away may be costly, if not impossible.

Equity vs. Appreciation

So, is a home a good place to "stash the cash"?

Let's assume the **Free-n-Clears'** home is worth $300,000 today, and they bought it seven years ago for $229,000. Add about $25,000 in capital improvements, and the rate of return would be in the neighborhood of 2.41%. Would you consider that a good return on an investment? How does this return compare to the inflation rate? What if you get caught in a position where the market value is going south? With your return negative, it would make little sense to put extra money into a home that is worth less than you paid for it.

Now let's assume the **Free-n-Clears** $300,000 home purchase is worth $530,000 just four years later. That would represent over a 15% return on investment! How much would their home sell for if they had put down $0? The same. How much money you have in your home does not increase the value of the home.

Remember the **Owe-it-Alls** live right next door to the **Free-n-Clears** and the only difference is that they kept their money in "Their Bank," and made monthly mortgage payments. How much would their home sell for? $530,000. However, during this time, their money has been earning interest, they have received tax deductions and, perhaps most importantly, they have had access to their money.

Your home appreciates the same whether you have it paid off or financed 100%.

Understanding the Spread

You are probably thinking that if you financed more, your payments would be higher, and that would be correct. This part of the discussion has to do with a concept we called the spread: what you can earn on your money and what you have to pay to use the bank's money.

As of the writing of this book, mortgage rates are available around the 6% mark—which is historically very low, and as the economy struggles they are likely to go even lower. A $300,000 mortgage at 6% for 30 years would carry a monthly payment of $1,799. Total principal and interest payments would be $647,515 over 30 years, and when we consider the opportunity cost to carry that mortgage, the overall cost would be $1,806,773 ($1,799 a month compounded at 6% for 30 years).

To better understand the spread, let's assume that you have $300,000 in your possession today. You are trying to decide whether you should pay cash for your $300,000 home, leaving you with no payments, or invest the money and secure a mortgage and make payments.

The **Owe-it-Alls** assumed they could average an 8% return on their money over the 30-year period, and their $300,000 would therefore grow to be worth $3,280,719. Their mortgage payments would be $1,799 a month and the opportunity cost on those payments would be $1,806,773. They would then end up with the *difference*—which is known as the "spread."

To calculate the spread, you must at least know what interest rate you would need to earn in order for you, rather than the bank, to control your money. The mortgage rate minus your tax bracket will give you your net cost to borrow. You then compare your net cost to borrow with your investment return potential.

If you can earn a higher return than your borrowing rate you will make money.

Net Cost to Borrow

Suppose the **Owe-it-Alls** investment rate is the same as their mortgage rate. Assume their mortgage rate is 6% and they do not feel they can net more than 6% investing the money. Many believe that if they cannot earn a higher return than their mortgage interest it makes good financial sense to pay the mortgage off. That appears wise, until you consider the mortgage interest deduction. If you fall in a 31% tax bracket, you would have to earn less than 4.2% to control the money rather than the bank (net cost to borrow). You have to answer this question for yourself: "Is 4.2% within my risk tolerance?" Remember—*you are not making money at 4.2%;* you have to *perform* that well just to break even to control the money.

> **If you qualify for mortgage interest deductions it reduces the investment risk required to control the money.**

Accelerated Mortgage Payments

Since most of us do not find ourselves in the financial position of the **Free-n-Clears** let us introduce a third couple: the **Pay-Extras.** Perhaps you will find your thinking more in alignment with theirs. The **Pay-Extras** choose shorter loan periods, and/or make extra principal payments with the goal to pay the mortgage off early.

Why do people choose a 15-year mortgage? Surveys conclude it is the *interest they think they will save.* The operative word here is: *think.* The *perception* is the shorter the loan the lower the cost. If that were true then paying cash would make the most sense. We have pointed out that paying cash for a home is not bad, but there is also opportunity cost to consider, as well as the control of the money.

The **Pay-Extras** might be surprised to learn that if they took the difference between the monthly payment of a 15-year and a 30-year mortgage, and invested that amount over 30 years, it would have the same value as paying off their mortgage in 15 years and investing that same payment amount from years 16 to 30. (This assumes the same interest rate and loan rate.)

> **It often takes increased risk, and requires more discipline to earn a given rate of return over a shorter period of time than a longer period.**

Interest Deductibility

What about tax deductions? *There are more tax deductions in the first 15 years of a 30-year mortgage than all 15 years of a 15-year mortgage*, assuming the same interest rates and loan amounts. Maximize all the deduction capabilities you can until you have the money to write one check to eliminate your mortgage.

Here is something further to think about: which deduction is of more value: your mortgage interest deduction, or the deduction on your Qualified Plan (401k) contribution? The mortgage interest deduction is a current known deduction, whereas the Qualified Plan deduction is a postponement of a future obligation. We will examine this in our next chapter.

Let's look at how the tax deduction affects each of our couples. The **Free-n-Clears** did not receive *any* deduction, because they had their home paid in full. Like many folks, the **Free-n-Clears** were also contributing to a Qualified Plan for their retirement. They did so believing they were saving taxes. These plans do not *save* taxes, they *postpone* them. And to which tax bracket are they postponed? That's a good question. *The only way to save taxes is to put money in the account at a higher bracket than the bracket at which you take it out.*

The **Pay-Extras** also contributed to their qualified retirement savings account at work to get a deduction on their taxes, but lost the very deduction they received at work because of the deduction forfeited on their mortgage interest. The interest deduction was even more valuable than their Qualified Plan deduction because it is a known amount today. On one hand the **Pay-Extras** say they want a deduction (retirement plan) but on the other they give up the deduction available by paying off their mortgage early.

The **Owe-it-Alls** believed that they could find an investment opportunity and earn at least enough to cover the mortgage interest after their tax deduction, allowing them to control their money. They only had to earn 4.2% (after tax), which they felt was well within their risk tolerance. They contributed to a 401k to get a deduction on their additional savings at work, while maximizing their deduction on their mortgage interest as well.

Hopefully, we have exposed you to several things that have perhaps challenged your thinking on the subject of mortgages; **there is definitely a lot to know.**

We are of the belief that *everyone should have his home paid off and paid off as quickly as possible.* That said, it does not mean that it is *wrong* to have a mortgage. What it does mean is that *you need to be able to "write the check."* If you have a mortgage of $300,000 and you have $300,000 in "Your Bank," your house is free and clear. The question is **not**, "Should I have my house paid for?" Both the **Free-n-Clears** and the **Owe-it-Alls** have their homes "free and clear." The real question here is, *"Are you going to BE the bank or a CUSTOMER of the bank?"*

In conclusion, let's look at several additional reasons you should retain control of your money in an account that carries with it the benefits associated with "Your Bank."

We suggest you become familiar with Form 1003, the Uniform Residential Mortgage Application. It is four pages in length, and is designed for lending institutions to determine if a person qualifies for a mortgage loan. To access the equity you have in your home, you have to apply and receive approval; you could even be turned down! How do you feel about having to *qualify* to access your own funds?

What Happens in the Event of a Disability?

The **Free-n-Clears** must complete the 1003 if they would like to access the equity they have in their home. In the event of a disability what will the bank say? **No**. The number one reason people lost their homes in

America in the past has been physical disability. Today foreclosures have taken center stage due to our current economic condition.

Upon review of the 1003 for the **Pay-Extras** what will the bank have to say in the event of a disability? Again—**No**. Remember—they still have their required payment due next month, even though they have been making extra payments in previous months. Now that the bank is in possession of their money, this couple will have to qualify to get it back. Does that sound like a safe position to you? Who is in control?

The **Owe-it-Alls** do not have to "qualify" to access their money. It is safely secured in "Their Bank," with no restrictions. It has not been until just recently in America that people understood how difficult gaining access to their equity could be.

What Happens If We Lose Our Job?

It would seem that if there were ever a time when one would need access to their money it would be when they lose a job. The **Free-n-Clears** must again fill out the 1003 and the bank will most likely turn them down. "When you get another job, call us," they might say, but what if the new job required a move?

The **Pay-Extras** want to withdraw some of the extra principal they have deposited while they look for a new job. The bank again most likely will return a negative verdict. If they move to a new line of work it may take two years before the bank will give them serious consideration again.

The **Owe-it-Alls** are still earning interest on their money, and they have full access to their principle, deposited in "Their Bank," and can withdraw what they need, with no questions asked, until they can get back on their feet.

What Happens if Mortgage Interest Rates Go Up?

The **Free-n-Clears** may be forced to refinance at a higher rate to access their money than the rate they would have to pay if they had financed when rates were lower. Let's say they could get a loan today at 5% but in five years they have to withdraw their equity at 8%. They pay a higher price for the lack of control. Don't forget that mortgage rates have been as high as 21% in the past.

The **Pay-Extras** are in the same boat as the **Free-n-Clears**. If they have to refinance they may be forced to do so at a higher rate. Another place people have money is in their qualified retirement accounts, but there is no access to those accounts until age 59 ½ (without penalty). If they have a need for immediate cash (new car, medical emergency, college education, wedding), the home equity may be the only source available. Again they must qualify!

The **Owe-it-Alls** have their principal. If mortgage rates go up, they may be able to take advantage of higher market rates, since their net cost to borrow is less than their investment opportunity cost.

What if mortgage interest rates go down? The **Free-n-Clears** and the **Pay-Extras** will not even be interested; they would not think it affected them. The **Owe-it-Alls** will want to refinance and reduce their present payments, giving them more cash flow to put in "Their Bank."

What if property values go down? The **Free-n-Clears** find themselves at a loss. If they need to access their money, they will have less money available because of the decrease in property values. The **Pay-Extras** will most likely conclude that it makes little sense to continue putting more money into a house that is worth less and less each day—especially when they understand they will have to qualify to get it back should they need it. Our **Owe-it-Alls** are again in a position of control since they have the money in a safe place. If their home value goes down they still have access to their money. They certainly would not take their money and pay off a loan that is more than the underlying property is worth.

It's time to take our quiz one more time.

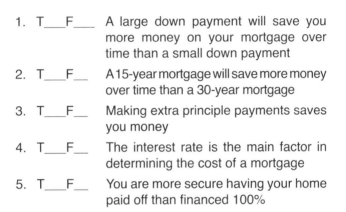

1. T___F___ A large down payment will save you more money on your mortgage over time than a small down payment

2. T___F___ A 15-year mortgage will save more money over time than a 30-year mortgage

3. T___F___ Making extra principle payments saves you money

4. T___F___ The interest rate is the main factor in determining the cost of a mortgage

5. T___F___ You are more secure having your home paid off than financed 100%

The answers are all false.

Granted, there is a lot to know about your mortgage and this discussion was certainly not an exhaustive overview. What you don't know may be more important that what you do know. If your thinking was challenged about this subject you should spend some time looking at your personal position. It is possible that more money will go through your mortgage than any other area in your financial life, including your retirement plan. This may be an area where you potentially could transfer money unknowingly and unnecessarily.

As we have said, we do believe you should have your home paid off as quickly as you can. But there is more than one way to do it. You can give more money to the bank that carries the loan, or you can put your money in "Your Bank" —the most powerful bank in the world.

Chapter **12**

Let's Talk About Retirement

And I'll say to myself, "You have plenty of good things laid up for many years. Take life easy; eat, drink and be merry." But God said to him, "You fool! This very night your life will be demanded from you. Then who will get what you have prepared for yourself? This is how it will be with anyone who stores up things for himself but is not rich toward God."
—Luke 12:19-21 (NIV)

Stu Stuckey was slowly beginning to realize the *relational* capital he had been transferring away in his relationship with Dina. He was a numbers guy—he understood the concept of capital—at least the monetary type. The fluctuating economy was driving him nuts, and he had become so focused on his company, his family's mortgage, future, and retirement, that he nearly lost sight of more important matters. For several days he had been working to repair an emotional breach between him and Dina, caused by a misunderstanding of the way he had handled their family mortgage funds—he simply had left her out. This had become too commonplace, and the practice had now caught up with him.

Dina, trying desperately to regain emotional balance, finally agreed with Stu's plan to meet with the financial advisor to have him review Stu's long-range objectives, particularly after scoring what he considered a "financial touch down" — elimination of their home mortgage! Secretly, Dina hoped the counselor would convince Stu there was plenty of money in reserve, so he could be a little more generous about funds for some of the projects that were important to her.

Stu finally connected with the financial advisor as agreed. What he had hoped would be total confirmation, "thumbs up" approval of his well-crafted plan, took a totally divergent path! Would you like to know what happened? He's on the interstate on the way home; we might be able to "tune in" on his thinking.

"I can't believe what he told me! I really thought I had a better handle on things.

"I guess I was ignoring the fact that I had a *partner* in my retirement plan. I've been deferring taxes to potentially pay them at a higher tax bracket later, and that's probably going to eat up more than a third of the value!

"And I was so proud of myself by paying off our house early. I sure didn't know that would keep us from getting any financial aid from the government for the kids' education. I guess we're going to have to come up with that some other way. Home equity? Yeah, right! I just put it in there, and now it's going to cost me to get it back out?

"And our 401k! Holy cow! I've put all that extra money in there thinking I was saving taxes. I never thought of the possibility that taxes could be HIGHER when we retire. How did I miss that? How did he put that? 'You don't **save** taxes — you only **postpone** them...'

"How am I going to explain this to Dina? There is no way we can get that car, let alone afford any of those other projects she is so eager to get started with. I feel awful. What am I going to do?"

Can you identify with Stu? How confident are you that your "plan" is a good one? *If what you believed to be true about retirement turned out not to be true, when would you want to know?*

Keeping the Gold in the Golden Years

When one hears the word "retirement," words and pictures begin to swirl around in our brains. Many different images have been etched in our minds as financial institutions have bombarded the media:

- Moving to Florida to play golf, fish or live on a boat
- Sitting on the front porch, reading or playing with the grandchildren
- Traveling more: cruises and trips to see friends and family
- Purchasing a second home to "live the good life"

Interestingly, many of us have come to believe the myth that retirement equates to a lifestyle devoid of labor. While this may be a dream of many working Americans, total cessation of labor cannot be supported from the Scriptures. Retirement, as we envision it in Western culture, is simply not found in the Bible.

Obviously, there will come a day when we won't be able to do the same work we are doing today. In our economic system, we trade our life's energy and time for dollars, and at some point the time we have available will be lessened due to age or health issues. As one grows older in our culture, our wisdom and knowledge is replaced with youth. This is usually not because the value of the production of older citizens is diminished, but the cost to support an aging work force is more expensive.

We would like for you to consider "retirement" from a different viewpoint than what is perceived by most. As a follower of Jesus Christ, our retirement years should not look so different from our pre-retirement days. This presupposes a clear focus of life. We are all called as believers to carry the Good News about Jesus to the entire world: commonly referred to as the Great Commission. It seems there is no age restriction or economic financial position necessary in order to be thusly engaged throughout life. Retirement is not a destination; it is the means by which you get paid to support your lifestyle. And if your lifestyle is tied to the fulfilling of the Great Commission, the only thing that will change as you age is your pace and your pay—how you will fund those "Golden Years."

As examples: perhaps someone who has owned his own company in the past is no longer required to be actively involved on a day-to-day basis. Another person may have saved enough money to no longer make it necessary to trade his time for dollars. God has provided for most of us through our work and he told us that work is a good thing—he "invented it" when he put the first man in a garden and told him to tend it. Wisely laying aside money for our later years is a prudent thing, and one who does not do so may be presuming upon God's goodness. God has promised to take care of us and provide for our every need, but this does not mean that we are exempt from applying ourselves diligently to the labor assigned us in this world.

Defining Qualified Retirement Plans

The word "retirement" is most often associated with *qualified retirement accounts*. While there are many types of investments and accounts you can use to accumulate money towards your retirement, the focus of this chapter is **Qualified Retirement Plans.** The word "qualified" refers to the fact that the government has approved these types of accounts to **qualify** for *tax-favored treatment*, meaning contributions are deductible. Perhaps you would recognize qualified accounts by some of their common names: 401(k), IRA, SEP, Simple, or 403b, just to mention a few. These are all accounts that allow you to make a contribution or deposit today, receive a tax deduction for the contribution and defer the tax until the future, usually retirement. Thus the name "retirement account" has been applied to this grouping of products.

There are other accounts that allow you to put money away with after tax dollars and receive the future benefits tax free, such as the Roth IRA, which we will discuss later.

Countless Americans make contributions to qualified plans through their employers, making it easy to participate, since the money is deducted from their paycheck. Many of these plans have a feature where the employer matches the employee's contribution up to a specified amount. This is probably the most familiar type of qualified plan on the market.

You may feel you know all you need to know about how your retirement account functions. But, like Stu Stuckey, perhaps there are a few things that you did *not* know or have never considered. Our purpose in this discussion is not to make you an expert in retirement planning. We want to help you gain a deeper understanding of how these particular instruments are structured, and what rules govern them during the accumulation and distribution phases.

Your Silent Retirement Partner

Remember Stu's appointment with his financial planner? He suddenly realized the other player in the game had 100% control of the outcome! Uncle Sam had his hands deep in his pockets. Let's illustrate this.

What if you were to call your best friend and ask to borrow $10,000? And, amazingly, on the spot he wrote you the check! Two questions would immediately come to your mind:

ñ How much interest will I be charged for the loan?

ñ When do I have to pay it back?

Suppose your friend said to you, "I am doing pretty well financially, and I do not need the money right now. However, there will come a day when I will need it. When I know how much <u>I NEED</u>, I will then be able to calculate how much interest I have to charge you to get what <u>I NEED</u>. We can just work that out later."

Would you cash that check?

Absolutely not! But in the same way, millions of people are standing in line to do exactly that with the Federal Government in their qualified retirement accounts! *They are deferring a tax today to potentially pay it at a higher tax bracket in the future.* Deferring taxes appears to be a sound strategy, until you take into consideration the tax bracket into which those taxes are being deferred.

Qualified Plans do two things: they defer the TAX, and They defer the tax CALCULATION.

It is essential that you grasp this fundamental reality! During the accumulation years you are focused on *reducing your current taxes*, and these plans do exactly that. But they are not tax *savings* plans; they are tax *deferred* savings plans. There is a significant difference. A better word to help you understand this concept would be the word Stu's financial advisor used: "postpone." You do not *save* taxes; you simply *postpone* the tax to a later date. *The only way to "save" taxes would be to withdraw your funds at a lower tax bracket than you were in when you made the contribution.*

There are some obvious questions that may occur to you at this juncture. The first is, "What tax bracket will I be in when I retire?" **The myth is that you will be in a lower tax bracket.** If you were to retire in the same tax bracket, it would mean that *you were not a saver,* and that you would not enjoy the same level of lifestyle you enjoyed while working. *The sad truth is that many people find themselves in higher tax brackets during their retirement years than they anticipated.* Remember that your income in the future must be higher to maintain the same standard of living because of **inflation**. This means you would be living the same way you always lived, but it's going to cost you more.

The next question is, "What deductions will I have when I retire?" Typically, by this time of life, children have all moved out (hopefully) and the mortgage is paid off. The tax deductions you once received for having children under your care, and mortgage interest deductions are suddenly gone: just in time for you to start taking money out of your qualified retirement accounts. *With no deductions, you will have to pay taxes on 100% of the money withdrawn at ordinary income tax rates.* That may not have been as apparent to you as we hope it is now.

That does not mean you should not save money in a qualified plan. People do things without really knowing why, or simply because everyone else is doing it. We are amazed at how many people reach retirement age believing they will owe no taxes on the money they have accumulated in their qualified retirement plans.

To illustrate further: if you deposited one dollar in one of these qualified accounts, you would conclude you had one dollar. *But that would not be true.* **You would not have a dollar; you would have one dollar _minus_ your future tax bracket.**

Assuming a current 30% tax bracket, if you withdrew your dollar today, the government would deduct their 30 cents, leaving you with 70 cents (exclusive of the 10% early withdrawal penalty). In a qualified account the government simply says, "You can pay the tax later." Assuming you remain in the same 30% tax bracket you were in during your years of contribution, when you retire, the government will want their 30 cents *at interest* and you will get your 70 cents *at interest.* Here is the harsh reality: *if the government decides they want more they simply raise the taxes and your portion of the account is further diminished.*

Tax Savings: Real or Apparent?

We have talked repeatedly about opportunity cost in previous chapters; the government understands this concept completely! Wouldn't it be wonderful if you could defer your taxes while working, and at retirement the government only required an amount equal to what you actually deferred. Unfortunately, that is not how it works.

It is easy to overlook the government's share of your qualified plan, but they are not bothered by the fact that you never think about how much of it belongs to them, because you cannot access one dollar from this account before they get paid their portion.

If you are in a 30% tax bracket today, and since you do not know your future tax bracket, the best-case scenario is for every dollar you contribute to your account, you have an "apparent tax savings" of 30 cents. The reason it is an *apparent* tax savings is that unless you know the withdrawal tax bracket, it is impossible to determine if you are actually saving any taxes. Again, the only way to save taxes would be for you to contribute money in a higher bracket than the withdrawal bracket.

We believe you should make contributions to one of these plans *if you are getting a match on your contribution*. If your employer does not match your contribution, then our counsel would be to think carefully before participating in a 401(k) plan at work. Though these accounts provide tax-deferred growth on your money—a good thing—they also prevent you from having access to your funds. These plans also do not enable you to create "Your Bank" as we have discussed in earlier chapters. For some individuals, lack of access is a positive thing, due to their inability to manage and control the funds. However, there is more to consider on this issue.

For example, the vast majority of the world drives to work in vehicles that have been financed. Are you able to see the problem with that picture? You are *earning* interest, but at the same time you are *losing* interest. Since you have no access to the money in qualified plans until age 59 ½, the lack of access can cause you to lose money in other areas. If the majority of your funds are tied up in an inaccessible account, you may be forced to borrow and pay finance charges so you can even get to work! The money you are losing in interest on your car payment is diminishing and reducing the return you are getting on your retirement savings.

As we pointed out earlier, most Americans will transfer more money away financing the cars they drive to work than they will have amassed in their lifelong savings. It is important that you make certain you are not losing today the very gain you expect to have in the future. The tragedy for so many is that by retirement age, more has been lost along the way than has accumulated in their retirement accounts.

It makes very little economic sense for you to take unnecessary risk in funding your retirement accounts, while transferring away interest on credit cards and consumer financing of automobiles. If you receive a match on your retirement contributions, don't do something in another area that would derail your employer's generosity. One way to look at the match is that the contribution from your employer will hopefully cover the future tax liability, and you will receive your contributions at interest. *Thank you very much, Mr. Employer!*

If you do not receive a match on your contributions into one of these accounts, it would be foolish for you to make car payments or pay interest on credit cards. It becomes a wash: an equal amount of money you are saving for your future could be lost in your poor spending habits today.

Qualified Plans vs Roth Plans

What about a Roth IRA or Roth 401(k)? These are good vehicles for the accumulation of retirement funds as well; however, *you do not get a tax deduction when you make a contribution.* Here is the difference between a traditional qualified plan and a Roth Plan: you must pay the taxes up front on your contribution, *but the interest earned in the account comes out tax-free.* This can be a good thing.

Which type of plan should you have? If you are of the opinion that you will be in a *lower* tax bracket when you retire than you are in today, then you should contribute to an ordinary IRA or traditional qualified plan. If you think you will be in a *higher* tax bracket when you retire, you would want a ROTH type account that will allow you pay your taxes today at a lower bracket, and take the money out when tax brackets are higher. The question is, "Are you a saver or a spender?" Your answer will have a substantial impact on which tax bracket you will find yourself in at retirement.

Two Types of Pain

It is important that you understand how your lack of attention to this issue of planning for your retirement might impact your future. *Will you thank God for his provision during your productive years, or curse him for your lack of discipline during your retirement?* Saving does bring with it an element of pain. It has been said that there are two types of pain: the pain of *discipline* and the pain of *regret.* Which will you choose?

How does what you do with your retirement account impact your relationship with your spouse? The premise of this book has been that you and your spouse are different, and those differences were *designed by God* to **help** you in your relationship not **harm** you. You may find yourself different from your spouse when it comes to spending and saving—living for today or living for tomorrow.

If you are the **Saver** in your relationship, you may find yourself consumed with the issues of your future and the question, "Will we have enough money when we retire?" How does that impact you when your spouse is more of a spender? Do you work your differences out together, or do you isolate yourselves from one another in this area?

If you are the **Spender** in the relationship, do you value your differences and see it as a blessing from God to help you, or do you see your spouse as someone in the way of you getting what you want? Can you see how important it is for you to understand your divinely designed difference when it comes to money in general and retirement in particular?

Is your retirement strategy one that unites you or divides you? It is quite possible that you could have been married for years without having a serious conversation with your spouse about plans for the future. Do you judge those differences in your spending and saving habits or have you learned to honor them? When you speak of your spouse's position, is it out of respect and honor or disdain and ridicule?

"We can't ever get ahead, because as soon as we get any money put away my spouse finds some foolish thing to spend the money on."

"We never go anywhere or do anything because my spouse is consumed with having enough money when we retire. I want to have enough to retire as well, but I would also like to live along the way."

In financial counseling, one of the most positive things we hear about retirement plans at work is: "They take the money out of my check so that I do not even see it. If I had access to the money I would just spend it." If you find yourself in this position, then by all means allow your employer to help you with the discipline of saving. But this word of caution as well: although you may be doing something at work, this alone may not be sufficient to sustain you during retirement years. You need to determine the lifestyle that will be required in your future, and make sure you are doing what you need to do today to be where you want to be tomorrow. To have enough resources at retirement take discipline and effort, and it is important that you and your spouse *act as one* when it comes to managing your money. Too often we run into couples that have left the management decisions of their money to their spouse and are shocked to find out that they are not in the position they hoped they would be.

If you thought there were opportunities for division during the accumulation phase of life, understand those opportunities will be even greater in the distribution season! It is important for you and your spouse to have a clear picture of your God-given goals for the Golden Years. Don't end up like Stu on the interstate, having a mental conversation with yourself—one filled with regrets.

We opened Part 2 of this book, the Money Section, with references to the dangers associated with wealth in general. Scripture has much to say about money, and we wanted some of those pitfalls clearly understood as we threaded our way through the forest of credit cards, mortgages, debt and retirement. Like a bookend, we want to shore up this section with another foundational piece on work, before we tie everything together in our final chapter.

We believe confusion arises when people do not understand why they are working so hard each day. Is it simply to accumulate wealth so you can live comfortably at the end of your days? Not so, according to the writers of Scripture. Without God in the equation, money matters don't really matter. Understanding **why we work** is far more important than **work itself**.

Chapter 13

Why Go To Work?

Do not labor for the food which perishes, but for the food which endures to everlasting life.
— *John 6:27 (NIV)*

We began this book by examining the "Book of Beginnings," Genesis, in relation to God's divine design for marriage. The Stuckeys and Baileys have served to illustrate the common struggles couples in America face, given the pressures of our way of life. In the same way God had a plan for Adam and Eve and their *marriage*, he also had a plan for their *occupation*. God put Adam in the Garden of Eden "...to **work it** and take care of it" (Genesis 2:15 NIV). So we see that one of the first things God did with Adam was to **give him a job**, signifying how important the issue of work is to him. In this chapter, we want to focus on the subject of work and our attitudes toward this dimension of life— particularly in relation to how it affects our marriages. If what you believe about work turns out not to be true, don't you want to know it?

It is obvious that our two couples have experienced various levels of marital conflict stemming, in part, from their misunderstandings of their differences and how to value their unique strengths to produce a stronger relationship. Another failure for them, and many of us, is simple lack of time together in order to maintain enjoyment, vitality, communication and intimacy within their relationship.

For each of them a large part of their day is given to work, and it has been slowly sapping not only time but also energy from their marriages, to the point of sabotaging their priorities, both personal and professional. *We contend that most people work for the wrong reasons, just as we suggested in chapter 2 that most marry for the wrong reasons!* Tiger Bailey is a prime example of working for the wrong reasons! A driving force of his life—that for which he seems to live and breath—is to "get ahead and succeed." The question is, "Get ahead of whom?" or "Succeed at what?" Who defined success for him? His desire to climb the ladder of success was a major contributor to bringing his marriage close to the brink of failure. He may arrive at the top of the ladder only to find it leaning against the wrong wall!

The question we are posing, "Why Go To Work?" may at first glance seem rhetorical. The most obvious answer to this question is, "to make a living." Actually, there are many factors producing a mind-set that holds out the promise that work will bring about wealth, prestige, esteem, purpose, value and a grandiose lifestyle. This conviction is another of the lies we have referred to in this book.

The reasons for which we go to work are derived from many sources: our parents and families, the culture, our own greed, lack of Godly role models and the lure of Madison Avenue and Wall Street. Besides those reasons listed above, are there other—more substantive—reasons to go to work? We have made three discoveries about work in the Bible, and after reflecting on each of them, we will turn our attention to five major *principles* of work.

Here are three clear Biblical reasons why we should go to work:

1.   Work was commanded by God (Genesis 2)
2.   Work is our arena for service and ministry (Matthew 6)
3.   Work affects our reward in heaven (1 Corinthians 3)

God's Commandment to Work

Sadly, in America, work has become that component of life that truly defines us: most derive their sense of identity, fulfillment and self worth from their jobs. The first question we ask of a stranger is, "What do you do?" Think of it: are we human BEINGS or human DOERS? Does God really want us to enter the marketplace simply because we have no other way of figuring out who we are and why we exist? Is life about money and self, or about God? Scripture sheds light on the difference between the cultural view of work and God's view of labor and leisure. Our first proposition is that God has given us work to do, and it is therefore intended for our ultimate good.

Here again is the Genesis account of man's first occupation:

> *"The LORD God took the man and put him in the garden of Eden to till it and keep it."*
> — *Genesis 2:15 (RSV)*

In effect, the first commandment ever given to man by God was, "Go to work!" Work is not a *suggestion*, but a deliberate *imperative*, and, therefore, holds high value and meaning. God has never rescinded this directive. Incidentally, because the command is still binding, and there is no reference to "retirement" in the Bible, why does our culture practice the total cessation of labor? This is yet another lie—that retirement is the *ultimate purpose in life* and something to be desired. Did the Creator really mean for us to eliminate labor in order to "kick back, play golf and travel?"

It is not *whether* or not we work, but *why* we work that is at issue. We work because God commanded it; we work because it glorifies him; and we work because it is intended for our good.

Increasingly, men and women are spending more and more time pursuing their careers in order to escalate the level of their lifestyles. Couples are marrying later in life in order to accumulate wealth before "settling down." Remember, the Stuckeys and the Baileys are both two-income families and reduction of lifestyle seems never to be an option. UPWARD mobility is the name of the game! We have never seen a book written on DOWNWARD mobility—have you?

So, in the homes of our favorite families, the alarm goes off, the coffee is brewing, headline news comes on, and relationships are ignored. Off to work we go, ostensibly to "make money to pay the bills" (or is it the "frills?"). Perhaps the Baileys and Stuckeys, like us, go into the world to make money: the more the better. However, there are better reasons to venture beyond the confines of our own fortresses of safety and security.

An Arena (Platform) For Ministry

Remember the passages in the Bible which we refer to as the "Great Commission?" With statements like those in Matthew 28, *"Go into the world and make disciples..."* Jesus addressed his disciples, who represent ordinary people like all of us. These were not professional clerics; there was no institutional church as yet. Notice what Jesus did NOT say. He did not say, *"Go into the world and make money,"* nor did he command us to, *"Go into the world and build successful careers or businesses."*

It isn't "ministry versus our job" but, rather "ministry or service in the *midst* of our job or business." A better translation of the passage above is, "...as you go make disciples." It is a matter of focus or mind-set. In fact, in another verse Jesus said In the same way, let your light shine before men, that they may see your good deeds and praise (glorify) your Father in heaven." (Matthew 5:16 NIV)

The challenge facing us is that we are called to be light in a dark world and commanded to work in an environment that has a completely different value system. Often the temptation to conform to the world is so subtle we can find ourselves off track without even realizing it—becoming *entangled* by the values, priorities and systems around us. When we overlook the needs of others it is easy to occupy ourselves only with the insatiable desire to meet our own needs. The opposite pole is to seek to become light—looking to the needs of others above our own—in the world about us. Did you notice in either of our families any hint of focus on the needs of others?

By adopting a faulty definition of success, we develop an accumulation mentality toward wealth, and finally, an addiction to work. This addiction is inevitable when we view the workplace as the source of the wealth we need to shore up our significance and to maintain the level of lifestyle we have come to enjoy and expect.

If our relationship with God is not plainly evident to those around us in the workplace, there is a good chance we are going to work for the wrong reasons.

God commanded us to work. He sends us out to serve and minister, but thirdly, he points beyond the present to a future estate.

Reward in Heaven

When we are young, we rarely think of the future, financial, spiritual or otherwise. Heaven is a difficult concept to grasp. The Scriptures teach that a personal relationship with Jesus Christ is the only assurance of entrance into that place called heaven (Romans 3:23; 6:23; Revelation 3:20; 1 John 5:11,12, et al.). What that place will be like for each of us is even more difficult to envision. However, you may be assured from Scripture that *there will be a difference in heaven* between those who have been faithful to God and those who have not:

> By the grace God has given me, I laid a foundation as an expert builder, and someone else is building on it. But each one should be careful how he builds. For no one can lay any foundation other than the one already laid, which is Jesus Christ. If any man builds on this foundation using gold, silver, costly stones, wood hay or straw, his **work** will be shown for what it is, because the Day will bring it to light. It will be revealed with fire,

and the fire will test the **quality of each man's work.** *If
what he has built survives, he will receive his* **reward.** *If it is
burned up, he will suffer loss; he himself will be saved, but
only as one escaping through the flames.*
— 1Corinthians 3:10-15 (NIV)

Emphasis has been added to highlight the connection between work (or how we live our lives), it's quality, and the reward awaiting us in heaven for that kind of faithfulness. God's evaluation or judgment of us is based on our faithfulness to the opportunities he presents us in life. If we are unable to put in abeyance our financial instincts for survival, we jeopardize our eternal future: not whether we will *go* to heaven, but how we will be *rewarded* in heaven. This is a truth underemphasized among God's people. The fact that there will be a difference in heaven is abundantly clear: some will receive greater or lesser degrees of reward. WHAT those rewards will be is not as clear and a subject for further discussion.

We seem to concentrate on becoming the conductor on a money train. We view life as a cash machine needing oiling. Rather than focusing on earthly lifestyle, as we mature in Christ we should turn our attention toward our heavenly lifestyle! Eternity is our true home—this earthly existence is not. The Bible describes us as "strangers and pilgrims" on the earth (1 Peter 2:11), but it is easy to live as though we are permanent residents. Our attitude ought to be more like living in a motel room. We don't move in, unpack and begin to redecorate the room! We realize we will only be there a short while. So it is with life.

According to these three reasons for going to work, what principles should we build our belief system on as we seek to repair our faulty foundations? What advice can we give the Stuckeys and the Baileys as they view their daily jobs and the need to "make a living"? In addition to understanding differences and how to mesh them harmoniously, would it further serve to reduce tensions and improve communication if they understood how God views their work?

How about you?

Mixed Signals

The Scriptures appear to give mixed signals regarding labor. Prior to the Fall of man in Genesis 3, and as we have previously pointed out, God placed Adam in the Garden of Eden to "till it and keep it" (Genesis 2:15 RSV). So God gives us work to do, but later we read that man toils and travails in his labor (Genesis 3:17-19). Let's call this work vs. labor. Before the Fall, work seems to be good: it must have given some pleasure and without a doubt, it glorified God. After man sinned, it became laborious—with it came pain and frustration.

So work is good and work is not good. Even Solomon, the wisest man in the Bible struggled to unite these opposing ideas:

> Then I realized that it is good and proper for a man to eat and drink, and to find satisfaction in his **toilsome labor** under the sun during the few days of life God has given him—for this is his lot.
>
> —*Ecclesiastes 5:18 (NIV)*

Work brings satisfaction and yet it is toilsome. This is our lot. Here we see the frustration that Solomon senses from the toil of his labor balanced by the joy which his labor produces. So it ought to be with us. We ought to enjoy our jobs without being controlled by them, realizing work is sometimes boring and just plain hard!

Principles of Work

Principle 1
You do not work to earn a living.

The Greek work *merimnao* appears nineteen times in the New Testament, and six of them are found in Matthew 6:25-34. Matthew

6:25 is variously translated "take no thought for" (KJV) and "do not worry" (NIV). The question is, "take no thought" for or "do not worry" about what? Answer: what we are to eat, drink, wear, etc. In short: our living! The King James Version rendering of v.25 is basically "don't think about it!"—that is, don't allow your *occupation* to become your *pre-occupation*. The Apostle Paul writes, "And my God will meet all your needs according to his glorious riches in Christ Jesus" (Philippians 4:19 NIV). What an encouraging promise! All is all! All of what? All our *needs*. God says **he** wants to assume responsibility for providing our needs on earth, rather than our carrying that burden. Notice carefully that he promises to *meet* our needs but he also reserves the right to *define* those needs.

Contrast this with Matthew 6:33 where we are urged to concentrate our attention on "the kingdom of God and his righteousness." This underscores our second reason for going to work: it is an arena to extend the kingdom of God and serve people. We are to build God's kingdom and not our own. This glorifies God. The workplace becomes a "platform for ministry" much like that of a pastor, missionary or other vocational Christian worker.

Most conscientious followers of Jesus Christ, if asked whether or not they believe the words recorded in Matthew 6:24-34, would say, "yes." However, if you followed with the question, "Then why do you chase dollars in the marketplace?" they would most likely respond, "Because I am afraid that if I allowed God to determine my standard of living, he would set it lower than I want to live." Again, review reason number three for working: to determine our reward in heaven, or our *standard of living* in eternity. Most people would rather work hard, become successful, amass wealth, and give God the credit in hopes that it will appease him.

Tiger Bailey comes to mind again. His wife has been trying to gain his attention about his priorities, but he isn't hearing. Rather than listen to her, music of another kind is ringing in his ears. Kitty's dreams and desires are simply not on his musical score. He places his needs above hers (one wonders what he dreams about when he lays his head on the pillow).

Why is this first principle so important? If we do not understand our real reason for going to work, and we conclude we are responsible for meeting our own needs, we can end up *manipulating* people to our own ends rather than *ministering* to them (perhaps by introducing them to Christ)! We leave the sanctuary of our homes and churches only to extract a living from people, or put money in our pockets, not share our faith or put the needs of others before our own.

Principle 2
There is no cause/effect relationship between
how hard you work and how much you make.

In one sense this principle is merely a derivative of the first. If God is our provider, then how hard we work really makes no difference. The perception of the average worker, however, is that this simply is not so. Stu, Dina, Tiger and Kitty would all probably surmise that there is a direct cause/effect relationship between their effort and their paychecks; that is, a given amount of work produces a given result. At the end of the month, uppermost in their minds is the amount of the paycheck, and when they might realize a raise in their compensation. While this thinking aligns with the culture, it is not true from God's perspective. That reasoning does not take Divine Providence into consideration. Again and again God calls attention to this fact; Now this is what the Lord Almighty says: "Give careful thought to your ways. You have planted much, but have harvested little. You eat, but never have enough. You drink, but never have your fill. You put on clothes, but are not warm. You earn wages, only to put them in a purse with holes in it." (Haggai 1:6 NIV). Consider this passage from Deuteronomy:

> You will sow much seed in the field but you will harvest little, because locusts will devour it. You will plant vineyards and cultivate them but you will not drink the wine or gather the grapes, because worms will eat them. You will have olive trees throughout your country but you will not use the oil, because the olives will drop off. You will have sons and daughters but you will not keep them, because they will go into captivity. Swarms of locusts will take over all your trees and the crops of your land.
> — Deuteronomy 28:38-42 (NIV)

God is in control of your pay raises and cuts!

As an example of this principle: a farmer finds a piece of ground, prepares it, sows seed, waters and fertilizes it and, when the crop is mature, reaps and sells it. It is accurate to say that there is a *correlation* between the first and last steps, but the first does not *cause* the second. There are too many variables: drought, plague and market conditions. The farmer cannot boast as though he is totally responsible for the outcome. What did he do? He simply got the dirt ready and firmly pressed the seed below the surface. It is hard to brag about being a "good dirt turner" and "seed sower." He had to do his part and God did His. Likewise, the farmer's self-worth should not be in question because he had a poor crop.

One family buys a home, and it appreciates so rapidly that in five years they have tripled their money. Another couple purchases a home, only to find that it is in a depreciating neighborhood. Some people are born into wealth, some into poverty. It is God who raises one up and puts down another (Psalm 75:6,7). People everywhere understand this is how life is lived. We cannot assume that poverty in emerging nations is due solely to people's lack of hard work!

When the Stuckeys and the Baileys step out of their homes in the morning and enter the world of work, they need to understand they are to work with excellence and diligence, since, as we have said, God commands it. We are to do everything to the glory of God (1Cor. 10:31). But we must work for the right reason, and we must not succumb to the erroneous reasoning that our work has *caused* the production of wealth. The Book of Colossians reminds us, "Whatever you do, work at it with all your heart, as working for the Lord, not for men" (Col. 3:23). We should plan, but we should realize that God retains the right to override our plans (Proverbs 16:9).

In summary, this principle teaches that arrogant men cannot come before God some day and say, "I did it all with the might of my own hands." Clearly, the Bible teaches us that we are to work hard, not to store up treasure for ourselves, but rather to glorify God in word and deed. The cause/effect relationship has more to do with our desire to see God glorified by integrating our faith and ministry with our jobs.

Principle 3
There is no intrinsic value in the product of your work.

The word to underscore in this axiom is *product*. There is a difference between *product* and *process*. The product of Stu's work, versus Tiger's work, for example, may have different degrees of *utilitarian* value, but no *intrinsic* value. Stu's work may help someone in a measurable, practical way, while Tiger's may deal more with mental work, which is not as tangible.

Here is another example: an automobile has value in that it helps one get from point A to point B. Yet in chapter 3 we saw that it became the topic of serious debate between Stu and Dina while they were contemplating the purchase of a new one. They lost sight of the difference between utilitarian and intrinsic value. The vehicle — the *product* of someone's work — is nothing but a piece of rusting metal that will some day be relegated to a junk yard! We have dealt with the mistakes we make in paying for and operating these cars and the painful problems they produce for us. Peter reminds us of the fate of the "things" we amass in life in this verse:

> ...and the earth also and the works that are upon it will be burned up...
> — 2 Peter 3:10b (RSV)

Think of it: God is so impressed with the products we spend our lives producing that he promises some day to "torch" them! What then IS important? The *process* of work, or why you do what you do and the way in which you do it. This might be called the *focus* of life, and it is what we referred to as reason number three for going to work: determining reward in heaven (see again 1 Corinthians 3:14,15).

God may assign value to the product of our work simply because he loves us—because we are his children. It is based on our relationship with him. We, for example, assign value to *our* children's work because they are *our* children. We post their artwork on our refrigerators even though they aren't masterpieces to anyone other than us. When they have forgotten them, we throw them away. Think about your reaction to that statement. Throw our children's "first" artwork in the trash? No way! Does it not give us a profound picture of what we consider to be of value? It was not the product, but the child, and the labor of love that was inestimable. Likewise, God assigns value and appreciates the beauty of what we produce—since he gave us the gifts to produce them—but expects us never to lose sight of the fact that they will some day "BURN!" That fact alone ensures we keep life in perspective: the product of work is *temporal*, the process of work is *eternal*. This dichotomy of Scripture is an important one to bear in mind.

Again, why is this important? The danger here is that if this is not kept uppermost in our minds, we can give our lives to the production of temporal things (buildings, art, or other products), rather than eternal things (people). God is constantly tweaking our value systems, and that is why he encourages us to "labor for things that do not perish" (John 6:27)—that is, for things which transcend time into eternity.

Principle 4
Significance is not found in the kind of work you do.

This is a HUGE problem for us Americans. The last several decades have been marked by a major identity crisis: people are searching desperately for a sense of self-worth and purpose. The popularity of books and articles on purpose attest to this. Two timeless questions have again emerged in this generation: "Who am I?" and "What am I for?" (How many times have you heard someone say, "I can't seem to find myself?")

Why are the Stuckeys and the Baileys both two income families? One reason, obviously, is financial. Their lifestyles—standard of living—have been constructed around two paychecks. In that sense, they are both "stuck!" Another reason might be the issue of significance. Kitty thinks about what it would be like to give up her job, move to the country, and start a family, but leaving her company would rob her of her self worth. Tiger barely pays any attention to her as it is, and she fears her parents would be disappointed, feeling that she would be wasting her life and her education.

Dina tried being a stay at home mom early in their marriage but discovered she would never have any of the things in life she wanted on a single income. Besides, she feels "needed" at work, just as Kitty does.

We are not saying these women should not work outside the home; the issue is identity. But, ilt is not only these working wives who are deriving their worth from the wrong source; most men in the marketplace define themselves through job titles, business cards, organizational charts and the size of their offices! A measure of the truth of this is to ask ourselves this question: "How do I feel about myself when I am unemployed?"

It seems that, throughout history, this same identity problem has plagued us. Rather than relying on God, we have looked to our jobs to define our significance:

In Robert Bolt's play, **A Man For All Seasons,** there is a scene in which Richard Rich, an ambitious young man, asks Thomas Moore for a position in the court of Henry VIII. Instead, More tells Rich that he should become a teacher, not a courtier—*"You'd be a good teacher." Rich objects: "And if I were, who would know it?" More's response is illuminating: "Yourself, your friends, your pupils, God; pretty good public that!"*[1]

We are called to play in God's great drama, and it is not the size of our role but the audience to whom we play that makes the difference. If we are ambitious to be impressive before people, we will never attain the true significance we seek. Instead, significance is to be found in the simple ambition to be pleasing to God and to be faithful to his calling for our life, whether our part appears to be great or small. To allow our work to define us is to limit God, and to focus on insignificant things.

Later in Bolt's play, Rich compromises his integrity to attain political prominence, and betrays Thomas More through perjury in order to gain the position of Collector of Revenues for Wales. More is condemned through this treachery, and as Rich leaves the court, More tells him, "You know, Rich, it profits a man nothing to give his soul for the whole world… but for Wales?"[2] We were made for so much more than that.

Ken Gire, in his devotional writings, makes this observation:

Within us the dust of the earth and the breath of heaven are joined in a mysterious union only death can separate. But that relationship is often a strained one, for while the body is fitted for a terrestrial environment—with lungs to breath air and teeth to chew food, and feet to walk on dirt—the soul is extraterrestrial, fitted for heaven. It breathes other air, eats other food, walks other terrain. …we have a…mingling of blood within us from a lineage that is both human and divine.[3]

In the Book of Jeremiah God identifies three areas in which people look for significance:

> *Thus saith the LORD, Let not the wise [man] glory in his **wisdom**, neither let the mighty [man] glory in his **might**, let not the rich [man] glory in his **riches**: But let him that glorieth glory in this, that heunderstandeth and knoweth me, that I [am] the LORD which exercise lovingkindness, judgment, and righteousness, in the earth: for in these [things] I delight, saith the LORD.*
> — *Jeremiah 9:23-24 (KJV)*

Wisdom, power and wealth are not to be the sources of our identity. We are not significant to God because of the size of our investment portfolio, or the number of academic degrees we possess, or because we own a company or occupy a position of prominence. The world about us—the arena into which the Stuckeys and Baileys step each day—defines greatness in terms of these three factors: how much money we have, how smart we are, and many people we can control. We are led to believe that we are important only to the degree we excel in one or more of them. The Baileys and the Stuckeys need to understand that, in the economy of God, they are to boast not in any of these things, but solely in the fact that they know God and are seeking to do His work (Ephesians 2:10). We are of worth only because God *declares* us to be of worth, not because of our jobs!

Defining significance through money, intelligence or authority is one reason marriages across America continue to flounder. In chapter 2, we proposed that couples may easily *marry for the wrong reason*: lust/infatuation rather than love, and now we have suggested they might *go to work for the wrong reason*: increasing their riches rather than increasing the Kingdom of God.

Principle 5
You can contribute nothing to the work of God.

Is it possible to entertain the thought that we have something to offer to a God who is already quite self-sufficient? The word "contribute" connotes giving, furnishing or supplying something of worth. Webster defines it as, "to give a part to a common fund or store; to lend assistance or aid to a common purpose." It conveys the idea of meeting a need. Does God have any needs? The Psalmist records this thought, "If I were hungry, I would not tell you, for the world and its fullness are mine" (Psalm 50:12 ESV). God does not need us. His children can *participate* in his work, but they can *contribute* nothing.

By allowing us the privilege of work, and by choosing to use us to touch others and help meet their needs, God is allowing us to have a "piece of the action." He is at work in the world, and we are doing him no favors by cooperating with him in this great drama called life. We might be tempted to think that "we make a good team—God and me." Or worse: God is "lucky to have me on his team!"

We need to understand that we are fortunate to have been allowed by God to act as his hands and feet in our homes, our neighborhoods, on our jobs, at school and even in places of commerce. We become the only picture of Jesus some people will ever see. Remember:

- ⁊ Money is not the issue. Maturity is.
- ⁊ Portfolios don't matter. People do.
- ⁊ Building your own kingdom is not the objective. Building God's kingdom is.
- ⁊ God doesn't need you. But he wants you.
- ⁊ You can't contribute. But you can participate.

Do not overlook this: you are of extreme value to God, not because of your performance, but because of his pronouncement. In fact, in God's economy, you are at the top of his list—so much so that he sent his son to die for you!

Those who do not understand the concept that they can contribute nothing to the work of God will be tempted to:

1. Establish goals without consulting God
2. Make them of primary importance
3. Ultimately compromise the commandments of God in an effort to accomplish them.

In one sad but true marriage, the husband said, "I want to serve God. My wife is not a follower of Christ, and hinders me in everything I do for God. She resents the money I give to God and the time I spend in ministry activities. She is a millstone around my neck. I have decided that I will divorce her so I can serve God better." Unfortunately, that is a common attitude and demonstrates that there are those who feel they have something to contribute to God's Kingdom. In an effort to serve God, they freely break his commandments.

Reflect on the Bailey's situation. What has led them to consider the option of divorce? Consider the five principles we have discussed and draw your own conclusions. What about the Stuckeys? Could their focus on money be changed by understanding the true meaning of work? What about you?

In summary, work existed before the Fall of man. It was good; it was God's command. After the Fall it was full of selfish ambition and became laborious. So our work is pleasant AND difficult but it brings glory to God. Ponder again Solomon's conclusions about our labors:

> *Behold, what I have seen to be good and fitting is to eat and drink and find enjoyment in all the toil with which one toils under the sun in the few days of his life that God has given him, for this is his lot. Everyone also to whom God has given wealth and possessions and power to enjoy them, and to accept his lot and rejoice in his toil—this is the gift of God.*
> *—Ecclesiastes 5:18,19 (ESV)*

Further, Paul writes to his protégé, Timothy, in 1 Timothy:

> *As for the rich in this present age, charge them not to be haughty, nor to set their hopes on the uncertainty of riches, but on God, who richly provides us with everything to enjoy.*
> *— 1 Timothy 6:17 (ESV)*

When God provides riches, enjoy them—share them! Just don't set your hopes on them; don't stake your life on money. It's uncertain. In many ways, it's dangerous.

We are called by God to "go into the world" (the marketplace, schools, manufacturing plants, neighborhoods) to live out our faith. We have followed two couples that have modeled for us in varying degrees an incorrect approach to marriage and money management. Not only have they been working for the wrong reasons, but also they are leaving one another behind by promoting their own ambitions for the use of the money that really comes to them from God. They are living as TWO rather than ONE.

Hopefully we have learned from their mistakes and from the advice we have given. What changes could you imagine if they applied our teaching? We have one last opportunity to tie together these strands of thought in our quest to ***"Avoid the Pitfalls of Love and Money."***

Chapter 14

One Plus One Equals One

Beloved, if God so loved us, we ought also to love one another.
—1 John 4:11 (KJV)

But lay up for yourselves treasures in heaven...
—Matthew 6:20 (KJV)

It finally happened: the "big one" — the titanic of all arguments. Not just another "heated discussion," it had been a gut-wrenching, 20-minute verbal exchange that left Kitty in total emotional shock. Ever since Tiger bought that new car, he had been acting strangely. He left early for work, came home late, spoke less and less to her, and, when they did converse, it revolved around how they seemed to approach *everything* in life so differently!

Then one night, he kind of freaked out. The option of divorce lingered faintly in the back of Kitty's mind from time to time, but she knew it was wrong. But now Tiger was talking openly about it, almost as though he had been planning it all along! He had stopped attending church with her months ago, so God wasn't even a part of his vocabulary right now. Kitty prayed and prayed, but nothing seemed to happen.

In distress, she had called her friend, Edith. Kitty trusted Edith, who was older, and she enjoyed the Bible study she led for younger women in the church. Edith suggested that Kitty make an appointment with the pastor to talk over some of her marriage problems. As daunting as that seemed, she made the appointment.

Kitty and the pastor met and were able to discuss the "rate of decay" of their marriage, and she was able to detail some of the unresolved issues they faced. Kitty was surprised to find out from Pastor Edwards that she and Tiger were not alone in their predicament. He said numerous other couples within their congregation were struggling with many of the same problems revolving around personality differences and money disagreements.

"Kitty, we are sponsoring a marriage conference here at the church in a few weeks, and I really think you and Tiger need to be here for this. You may have seen the poster for *Love and Money.*"

"Yes, I saw it, and I definitely will come, but I don't know about Tiger; he hardly speaks to me since that last big argument."

"Let me see what I can do about that," the pastor replied. "I think Tiger and I have enough of a relationship that he might listen to me. Don't think you are the only people that struggle with marriage and money problems. That's why we need this conference."

Meanwhile Back at the Stuckey Ranch

On the other side of town, another conversation is taking place, a little less heated, but nonetheless intense. Let's listen in.

"I told you I was sorry for not telling you about the mortgage money, Dina. After that meeting with the advisor, I just need more time to think to sort through our whole financial picture. I still don't know how we're going to finance all the projects you have on your list. There's only so much money to go around."

"Stu, waiting is always your answer. Why don't you just *talk* to me? It seems like all we ever do any more is *work* and *worry* about money. Our family nights have practically stopped, and how long has it been since we had a date night?"

Dina added quickly, "By the way, do you remember that *Love and Money* conference that the church is bringing to town? Stu, I really think we need to make that a priority, not just because I am part of the leadership committee, but because we need help in **both** areas: our marriage, and our money difficulties. I don't mean to say that you don't know a lot about money—after all, that's your job—but we might learn some things to help us out of this jam you say we are in. I have looked over the advance materials they sent us, and it really looks like something that would help me understand some of this stuff you have been trying to explain to me. What do you think?"

Stu reflected for a few moments, and then nodded his head approvingly. "I'm open to that. I hear there are a lot of younger couples who will be attending; maybe a little grey hair in the mix will round it out." He had not really planned to go, but since his meeting with the Financial Advisor, he knew he was going to need help in patching things up with Dina. On his drive home from that meeting, he realized he needed to pay a whole lot more attention to her. He definitely was not willing to sacrifice his marriage on the altar of money or the perfect financial plan.

Guess Who's Coming to the Meeting?

Love and Money: Biblical Truths to Transform Your Marriage and Finances. That was the title of the Participant Workbook Tiger and Kitty were each thumbing through as they sat down in the rapidly filling auditorium. That's right! Tiger had been persuaded by Pastor Edwards to attend with Kitty. For the last two weeks he had been spending a lot of time inside his own head: mulling over just how badly he had handled the car situation. "God thoughts" kept creeping in, and growing guilt over his argument with Kitty finally convinced him he had to do something drastic—even if it was church stuff!

So there he sat, reading the words, "What you know may not be as important as what you don't know." He glanced at the topics: differences, problem solving, risk, change; they all seemed scary. Tiger knew one thing for sure: *he and Kitty were about as different as two people could be.* He thought they held the number one spot!

And the money stuff: dangers, credit, retirement, and mortgages ... It was already starting to make his brain hurt! But he knew they had to do something! "If I dump her, will it really take away the pain and solve my problems?" he thought to himself.

Kitty sat silently next to her husband, hoping desperately for just a touch of his hand at this point. *"God," she prayed, "This is it.* If you don't help us today, it's all over, and I really don't want it to be over. I love this man, and I just want us to get along. Please, please do something special for us. I will do anything you ask me to do."

How many other couples prayed that same prayer that day? How do you think God responds to this type of prayer? We can learn an invaluable lesson from the prophet Hosea:

> *"Therefore I am now going to allure her; I will lead her into the desert and speak tenderly to her."*
> *—Hosea 2:14 (NIV)*

Life in general, and certainly marriage in particular, is never without pain or difficulty. A principle that may be garnered from Hosea 2 is, "God leads us—allures us— into the desert of difficulty in order to there speak truth in tenderness to us." In other words, **desolation is designed by God to produce desperation.** When we find ourselves at the corner of humble and desperate, God has us in the right location!

On that day, and because of that prayer, for Kitty and scores of others in that room, dramatic things began to happen. You see, at the conference the Baileys, the Stuckeys and all the other couples became aware that they were *different by God's design*: God had actually *intended* for them to be different. In fact, there was a law at work in their marriage—The Law of Differences. Most importantly, they finally began to understand that God had placed spouses together to *help* one another not *hinder* one another.

As they broke for lunch, Kitty struck up a conversation with the lady who had been sitting next to her, Dina Stuckey. They began to talk about the things they were learning, and Dina assured her that even though she and Stu had been married much longer, they still had many areas in which they needed improvement. This gave great hope to Kitty as she thought about the things she knew she needed to change.

"My husband told me at the first break that he thinks we have been leaving each other behind in a lot of areas of our marriage," Dina confided to Kitty. "You know, not really living as one, but as two."

"Like what, if you don't mind me asking?" Kitty responded.

"Well, first we're both busy: he's a financial officer in his company, and I'm a travel agent. We've got two teenagers and that makes for a busy household. And we have financial troubles. You'd think with two incomes we would be doing better. But Stu doesn't talk to me much about our money, and he's made a lot of decisions without me."

Kitty seemed surprised. "Wow, I thought we were the only ones that did that! Tiger just bought a car and didn't even ask me about it! We both work, too, but there never seems to be enough money to pay the bills. I suppose we all are going to have to make some major changes, huh?"

"Yes, we will. Let me encourage you, Kitty. Stu told me during our project time this morning that from now on we are going to talk over ALL our financial decisions. AND, what really excited me was that he said he realized he had not been taking my needs seriously. Believe me, that is a HUGE change!"

Dina added as a confession, "Kitty, I don't think I ever understood clearly that Stu was really looking out for our family's best interests—you know, trying to protect us. He's such a detail guy, and I just saw all that as a barrier to prevent me from getting some of the things I wanted. I hope you won't make that mistake."

Kitty was quiet as she looked away from Dina. Spotting Tiger, she submitted, "I see my husband is looking for me for lunch. I would like to meet Stu; do you think we could get together later this afternoon? This has been so helpful; I really want to continue this conversation."

Taming the Tiger

As they sat down for lunch, Kitty noticed that Tiger had chosen a secluded corner of the Family Life Center. He had not said much since the seminar had begun.

"Are you okay, Tiger," she offered, not really knowing what he was thinking.

"I'm okay, honey." He had not used any such terms of endearment for weeks. Kitty didn't know whether to be pleased or not; she was still hurting from the pain of their quarrel, and she was not ready to forgive him, though she knew she must.

"It's been a hard morning. I really can't eat much. I feel really beat up and guilty."

"What do you mean?"

"Well, Kitty, I guess in a nutshell I've been pretty selfish. I wanted the car. I want to look good and I want to be a big shot at the office. I hate to admit it, but I think about myself a whole lot more than I think about you."

Kitty had not eaten the first bite of her lunch. She was shocked. She stared at him, and she could feel tears coming to her eyes. She had never heard Tiger speak this way. Somehow, she knew something more significant than a shiny new car was about to pull up to her front door.

"Kitty, I have been thinking really hard; actually I think maybe God is talking to me. A car is just a car—a bucket of bolts. That opportunity cost thing on financing a car really floored me. I don't want the opportunity for me to have a new car to cost us our marriage. YOU are worth a whole lot more to me than something that is going to rust and wear out. I can't believe I actually thought I would be better off without you!

"Can you forgive me?"

"Of course. But Tiger…"

"Wait, Kitty," Tiger interjected. "You had better let me get it all out while I can. I think I learned something else this morning: we really are different, but that's not a bad thing. Maybe we can learn how to do this thing together like they were saying. I'm really sorry for what I've put you through."

"Tiger, I do forgive you, and I'm sorry I have been pushing you so hard on the house. Can you forgive me?"

"Yes," Tiger said softly as he laid his hand over hers.

"I am excited about the stuff we are going to learn this afternoon that will help us get our financial act together."

She continued intently, "I just want you to know that I will do whatever we have to do to keep our marriage alive. Our marriage is worth more to me than a house."

"I agree," honey. I know we need to get a handle on our finances, but I think we first need to go back where we started and concentrate on our relationship. If we don't get that straightened out, the rest won't matter. We've got to apply all that stuff about honoring our differences and becoming a great team."

"I'm very thankful to God that Pastor Edwards insisted that I come today."

"We'd better finish our lunch, the meeting starts in a half hour. By the way, who was that lady you were talking to—I've seen that couple at church before?"

"It was Dina and Stu … I think she said their last name was Stuckey."

The Heart of the Matter

God is in the forgiving and redeeming business. The story of the Prodigal Son in the Bible (Luke 15:11-32) gives us the picture of a Father always ready to welcome back a son or daughter gone astray. Just as there is no person who is ever beyond the realm of God's forgiveness, there is no marriage beyond repair. We have sought in this book to present the brighter and dimmer dimensions of marriage, and to assure you that God stands ready to apply grace and forgiveness to your marriage relationship as you, "Humble yourselves therefore under the mighty hand of God, that he may exalt you in due time…" (1 Peter 5:6 KJV). Peter continues in this vein: "Casting all your care upon him; for he cares for you (v.7). As you humble yourself and cast yourself upon God's mercy, he will "exalt" you, meaning he will redeem you, forgive you, and give you a fresh start. God is a father. He longs for his children to know joy and fulfillment.

May God bless your marriage, and guide you as you manage the money he entrusts to you. If we may be of further assistance, contact us using our web site below.

The Love and Money Seminar

The *Love and Money Seminar* is a one-day conference available to you and your church. Typically held on a Saturday, the Seminar is comprised of two parts. The first half of the day, "Different By Design," is the *Love* or *Marriage* portion of the day. Following lunch, "Money, the Great Divide" is presented. The topics addressed in this volume are covered in depth during the conference, as well as an opportunity to work through your individual Marriage Insights Profile. To make arrangements to bring *Love and Money* to your area, go to our web site **www.loveandmoney.org**.

Endnotes

Chapter 3 The Problem With Problems

1 Adapted from John Trent, Rodney Cox, Eric Tooker, Leading From Your Strengths (Nashville, TN: Broadman & Holman Publishers, 2004), 20-22.

Chapter 4 Do You See What I See?

1 Adapted from: John Trent, Rodney Cox, Eric Tooker, *Leading From Your Strengths* (Nashville, TN: Broadman & Holman Publishers, 2004), 20-22.

2 Oswald Chambers, *My Utmost For His Highest* (New York: Dodd, Mead & Company, 1935), 274.

Chapter 5 Let's Talk About Change

1 Adapted from: John Trent, Rodney Cox, Eric Tooker, Leading From Your Strengths (Nashville, TN: Broadman & Holman Publishers, 2004), 41-42.

2 David and Claudia Arp, 10 Great Dates to Energize Your Marriage (Grand Rapids: Zondervan, 1997).

Chapter 6 Who Needs Rules?

2 Adapted from: John Trent, Rodney Cox, Eric Tooker, Leading From Your Strengths (Nashville, TN: Broadman & Holman Publishers, 2004), 50-51.

3 T.S. Eliot, Choruses From the Rock (Quoted in various volumes.)

Chapter 7 The Mystery Of Differences

1 Kreider, Rose M. and Jason M. Fields, 2001. Number, Timing, and Duration of Marriages and Divorces: Fall 1996. Current Population Reports, pp.70-80. U.S. Census Bureau, Washington, DC

2 ibid.

Chapter 8 The Danger Of Riches

1 Source unknown.

2 Boyd Bailey, Money Motivated (Wisdom Hunters Right Thinking Devotional, October 14, 2006).

3 Chapters 8 and 9 are adapted from material previously published by Vision Foundation, Inc., Knoxville, Tennessee, and used by permission.

Chapter 10 The Danger Of Riches

1 Wikipedia Article, Willy Sutton, An Urban Legend

Chapter 13 Why Go To Work?

1 Quoted from a presentation by Kenneth Boa on *A Man for All Seasons*.

2 Ibid.

3 Ken Gire, *Windows of the Soul* (Grand Rapids, MI: Zondervan Publishing House, 1996), 48.

Index

Part 2 — Money The Great Divide